BLURRED LINES

Scott Hildreth

Published by
Eralde Publishing

Cover Design Copyright © Creative Book Concepts
Text Copyright © Scott Hildreth
Formatting by Creative Book Concepts

ISBN 13: 978-0692543351

DEDICATION

This book, entirely, is dedicated to my PA, Katrina Chadwick Wofford.

She has a full-time job keeping me in line. And she never ceases to amaze me.

Kat, you're the best.

PROLOGUE

Dressed in khaki trousers, a neatly pressed long sleeve cotton shirt, and work boots, the man stood arrow straight on the porch of the modest home as he reached for the doorbell. After pressing the button once, he leaned rearward and waited. From his utility belt hung various tools, a leak detector, and a roll of duct tape.

In a matter of a few seconds, the front door opened a few inches.

Upon recognizing the man as an employee for the gas company, the woman opened the door a little wider. The man lifted his identification card with his right hand as he clutched his clipboard with his left.

"Kansas Gas and Electric, Ma'am. We have a report of a severe gas leak in the area, and we've narrowed it down to the homes on this side of the block. I've got a leak detector, and I'll need to check your water heater and furnace for gas leaks. I should just be a few minutes," he said.

She raised her hand to her mouth as she gasped. "Oh my."

Still dressed in her robe and slippers, her reservation to allow him to enter the home was soon overcome by the fear of the unknown. She leaned forward and pressed her head between the door and the door frame.

"I'm sorry, I just woke up. The alarm..." She paused and gazed down at his boots. As she shifted her eyes upward, she continued. "I don't know what happened. The leak? Is it safe?"

The man shook his head. "No Ma'am, the leak has the potential to cause a severe explosion. That's why I'm here. We need to get this resolved, and quick. One spark could cause this entire block to be nothing more than a memory. I should just be a few minutes."

"Oh, alright," she said as she nervously pressed her hand against her unkempt hair.

The man removed the leak detector from his belt and raised it in front of him as he studied the small display screen.

"Come on in," the woman said as she opened the door.

Normally, she would be home alone this time of day. The alarm hadn't gone off, and the morning sun through the east window caused her husband to rise from his sleep, one hour later than normal. In the basement her child still lay asleep, unaware kindergarten class had long since started.

The man entered the home, quickly surveyed the room, and cautiously began to proceed walking toward the basement steps on his right side.

"I'll need you to show me where the water heater is," he said over his shoulder. "I assume it's here in the basement?"

"Yes, it's in the utility room," she responded. "I'm sorry but it's a mess down there."

A few feet before the stairway, he stopped and tilted his head to the side. The faint sound of the shower in the back bedroom was the only noise in the otherwise silent home. After a short pause, he turned to face the woman and cleared his throat.

"Is there water running?" he asked.

"Yes. My husband is taking a shower. He's late for work," she responded.

The man nodded his head and slowly turned around. He knew there was no place in his intricate scheme for a man. There was no turning back now. A small kink in his plan, but not one he wouldn't be able to overcome as long as he made quick decisions.

With lightning speed, he slid the lanyard of the detector along his forearm and swung his open right hand over the woman's mouth.

Her silence was crucial to his complete success. Failure, in his mind, was not an option. Although the husband's presence wasn't by design, he realized it would allow him to reach his goal in a more expeditious manner.

As he dragged the woman toward the back bedroom, his mouth curled into a shallow grin.

After taping the woman's mouth and binding her hands he walked confidently to the closed door which led to the master bathroom and positioned himself beside it. As the sound of the running water stopped, he held his hands at chest height and waited. He grinned and raised his hands slightly as he heard footsteps approaching the doorway.

They never should have denied my promotion to detective. I'm smarter and more cunning than any of them, he thought.

As the woman's husband stepped through the doorway and into the room, he gasped at what he saw.

And that was the last sound he would ever make.

RILEY

I pulled my car to the curb and stopped a hundred yards from the entrance, being careful to park in a location where no one inside could see what I was driving. I wasn't ashamed of my car, and in fact, quite the opposite was true; but it wasn't every twenty-one year old girl who drove an eighty thousand dollar car. It seemed as soon as someone realized what I drove, I was quickly labeled as a gold digger or a spoiled little rich girl, neither of which were true.

My former boyfriend gave me the car as a gift, and as much as he probably expected me to return it after we broke up, I didn't even consider it as an option. Putting a price on his abusive behavior would be impossible, but if I did, the car was a small price for him to pay for what he did to me over the four year period we were together.

Each time he touched me he later swore it would be his last, and for whatever reason any woman believes what her abusive boyfriend promises, I believed him. At first, I suspect it was because I was young, immature, and filled with false hope regarding what he would offer me long-term. At the time he was protective of me - sometimes overly so - but it was comforting to have someone care enough to be conscious of where I was going and who I was seeing. Over the next few years, I matured slowly, and his abusive behavior continued. When my level of maturity rose to a level which allowed me to question his behavior as abusive, I quickly did so.

Mentally, I drew a line in the sand on my twenty-first birthday, saying if the abuse continued, I would leave. He gave me the car as a birthday gift, and six months later slapped me so hard he knocked me to the floor.

The next morning I was gone.

The car did remind me of him, but forgetting Stephen entirely was close to impossible, as his face was plastered all over billboards throughout the city. My best option for forgetting him was changing where I spent my time, who I spent it with, and getting a much needed tattoo depicting my newfound intention of flying solo for a long, long while. My first six months of single life was easy, and I hoped the future remained just as simple.

There was very little risk in encountering anyone meaningful at ten o'clock in the morning at a tattoo parlor other than the overweight former sailor who I expected would tattoo the Latin phrase on my shoulder. As far as I was concerned, I should be able to go get a tattoo without exposing myself to anyone who would tempt me to be in another relationship. Although a relationship wasn't something I was afraid of or opposed to, I felt it was something I needed to proceed slowly with.

I glanced in the rearview mirror. Although my preference was to wear contact lenses, a severe scratch on my right eye - the result of his most recent slap - prevented me from doing so for at least another month. I removed my glasses, placed them on the passenger seat, and gazed into the mirror as I tossed my hair into a cute little mess.

Not knowing for sure how long the tattoo might take, I chose my most comfortable jeans, an open neck tee, sports bra, and my Chuck's. From what I had read on the internet, being comfortable was the most important thing about getting my first tattoo.

I walked along the rows of shops, peering curiously into the windows of each one as I passed. Living under Stephen's thumb for the last four years prevented me from seeing certain parts of the city; he preferred the more glamorous and glitzy east side to the artistic regions of down town.

With the early morning sun shining directly into my face, I walked along the sidewalk and toward the tattoo shop. As the warmth of the sun combined with my nervous stomach began to make me feel slightly uncomfortable, the flashing neon sign in the window to my immediate right caught my attention.

Blurred Lines.

A quick glance through the window and into the shop revealed the back of someone's head who was seemingly preoccupied with whatever he was studying. Having made my appointment over the phone and not knowing for sure what Blake looked like, I leaned into the door with little expectation of him being anything but a talented tattoo artist.

As I pushed the door open he spoke over his shoulder without turning around.

"Can I help you?" he asked.

I nodded my head as I glanced around the eclectically decorated shop.

The interior brick walls differed from the exterior brick in that they were covered with various pieces of painted canvas, framed watercolor paintings, and sketches on transparent paper. Dragons, winged serpents, snakes, flowers, and colorful fish surrounded me. As I seemed to lose myself in the colorful display of artwork, someone stepped between me and the wall I was ogling - well into my personal bubble.

As I began to step rearward and separate myself from the invasion, I realized in a matter of minutes he would probably be piercing my skin with a mechanized needle, and although it was nothing more than a tattoo, the experience would probably be an intimate one, bonding us together in what I hoped to be a long-term client-artist relationship.

And he meant no harm.

"Riley, my ten o'clock?" he asked.

I stood firm and shifted my focus from the dagger filled skull, nestled in a bed of roses, to the man standing at my side.

Covered in brightly-colored tattoos from his neck to his fingertips, he stood before me rubbing his hands together. As our eyes met, he extended his right hand and smiled, revealing much whiter teeth than I was prepared for.

He was far from the overweight sailor I had expected.

"Blake, I'll be doing your piece," he said.

I shook his hand, stared at his teeth, and smiled. "Riley."

He was tall and appeared thin at first, but as I studied him it became apparent his upper body was proportioned very nicely. The *Vans* tee shirt he wore - obviously one of his favorites - clung to his well-defined chest. Underneath his shirt, the definition of the cross he wore around his neck was apparent. I shifted my eyes along his body. Where the waist of the shirt met his belt, a few dozen holes adorned the faded black garment, clearly showing its age and his preference to wear it. Although I told myself not to stare, refraining from doing so was becoming increasingly difficult. He seemed to be, at least from what I was able to see, everything Stephen wasn't. He was attractive, yet cute in a boyish sense where Stephen was demandingly handsome. Instead of an expensive suit, he wore a tee shirt, sneakers and jeans. His hair wasn't cut perfectly, it was more perfectly un-cut. Instead of barking out orders, he stood and nervously rubbed his hands together. As I began reconsidering my recently adopted "single forever" mantra, I shifted my eyes upward until I met his gaze.

"So, what have you got in mind?" he asked.

Not knowing whether the slight growth of facial hair was the result of having hurried out of his house in the morning, or something he had done intentionally didn't really matter, it was the perfect complement to his strong jawline and made him even more attractive. He was the exact opposite of what I had expected.

I reached over my shoulder and patted my upper right back with my left hand as I nervously cleared my throat.

"'She flies with her own wings', but in Latin," I said.

He nodded his head and grinned.

"What?" I asked, feeling as if he knew something I didn't.

He cocked an eyebrow slightly. "You sure?"

"Uh huh," I responded.

He coughed a laugh and pointed upward. "Pull your shirt down over your shoulder and turn around."

"What?" I asked as I pulled the neck of my shirt past my shoulder.

He shook his head lightly as he twirled his index finger in a circle. I turned away from him and glanced over my shoulder, still wondering what he found funny about my request.

"What?" I asked again as he stepped closer.

I continued to peer toward him as he raised his hand. With my eyes fixed on his tattooed knuckles, he reached for my shoulder.

He traced along the skin of my upper back with the tip of his index finger.

"Here? Is this where you want it?" he asked.

Goosebumps rose along my arm. I closed my eyes and inhaled a choppy shallow breath. A simple trip to the tattoo parlor was quickly becoming a difficult walk down sensuality lane. I attempted to swallow, opened my mouth, and murmured a response.

"Yeah."

I wasn't necessarily prepared for him to touch me when he did so. I really don't know what I could have done to prepare myself, but whatever it was, I hadn't done it. He leaned forward, and although I suspected it was innocent, breathed into my right ear as he spoke.

"What I do to you is going to last forever, you need to be sure this is what you want before we go any further," he said.

You're doing this on purpose, aren't you?

His warm breath against my neck caused me to shudder. I opened my eyes, gazed out the window, and did my best to respond.

"Ah-lees Vo-lat Proh-pee-us," I said.

And the brief sensual moment I believed we were sharing was instantly severed as he began to laugh out loud.

BLAKE

Everyone has their own set of problems, and for me to claim I was anything short of normal would be a damned lie. Although I may not admit the extent of my concerns or issues with attempting to live a normal life to everyone, being honest with myself wasn't difficult.

Not really

I was an addict.

Anything that made me feel good had the potential of being a problem, and even realizing how broad of a swath the *anything* paintbrush covered, it was an accurate statement. Admitting my deficiencies allowed me to look at life through realistic eyes, identify possible threats, potentially bite my respective lip, and turn away before I allowed myself to get into any more trouble.

The last six months of my life had been difficult, but not impossible.

One day at a time was my new motto, and although living it proved difficult at times, I did my best. My profession didn't help matters, but I knew it would be impossible to find something I enjoyed more than owning my own tattoo shop. There was something about leaving a permanent mark on another person's skin that being a cop, selling cars, or landscaping yards couldn't compete with.

Tall, well-proportioned, and cute in an odd "I don't give a fuck what I look like" way, she stood facing away from me with the neck of her tee shirt pulled down over her upper arm. I glanced down at her ass. Prying my eyes away from it and attempting to keep from looking like a pervert wasn't easy, but I was doing my best.

Eventually I tore my eyes from her lower half.

"Alis volat propriis." It seemed I'd said the three words a thousand times in my short career of tattooing.

"Proh-pee-us," she said, mispronouncing the overused Latin phrase once again.

I stepped around her and shook my head. "I've done a few of these. Ah-lis woh-lat proh-pree-is is the proper pronunciation. The 'v' is pronounced like a 'w', and there's an 'r' in there. Believe me; it's not proh-pee-us."

She scrunched her nose and stared. "Are you sure?"

"I didn't mean to laugh, it's just that I've done like a hundred of these fuckers, and I'm quite sure, but let's have a look," I said as I motioned toward the monitor.

I reached for the keyboard and typed "She flies with her own wings in Latin" into Google's search window. The entire page filled with responses to my search, all spelling the phrase properly, and including an "r" as I had indicated.

"Well, there it is," I said as I waved my hand toward the screen.

She leaned over the counter, squinted, and stared at the screen. The crack of her ass and a very attractive torso exposed themselves as her shirt climbed up her waist. Guessing her age at mid-twenties, I was surprised she had waited as long as she did to get her first tattoo. It seemed most girls attempted to pop their tattoo cherry at roughly 16 years old, using their parent's consent as confirmation of their need to have their skin marked with whatever their adolescent mind dreamed up as necessary.

"Sorry, I didn't bring my glasses in," she said as she turned away from the monitor.

Oh fuck.

You wear glasses?

I glanced at Tyler and grinned. He pointed toward the street and nodded his head eagerly.

I shifted my eyes upward until my gaze met hers. "You wear glasses?"

Girls who wore bold thick-framed black glasses had been a weakness of mine since eighth grade when I was introduced to Mrs. Reisling, my well-endowed and very nearsighted home room teacher. She didn't wear low-cut tops as often as I wanted her to, but when she did, every boy in class tried to catch a glimpse of one of her three pound gravity defying tits. In hindsight, I was sure they were fake, the product of a very talented plastic surgeon. At the time, however, I viewed her as defined perfection, her bold school girl glasses included.

I stood, staring blankly at my new client, trying to imagine her wearing a bold black-framed Prada or maybe something from Cartier's newest "fuck me senseless collection". Three or four seconds later I was fighting with my subconscious self, trying to regain control over my rather eager - and always one step ahead of my brain - male anatomy.

I gazed beyond her and at the monitor as I desperately tried to think of something else to occupy my mind. Standing in front of her during her first session with a full blown hard on wouldn't be the welcome I expected she was prepared for.

Maybe during her second or third session I could rock a stiff cock, but certainly not on the first.

"I can't see without them, but I hate to wear 'em," she said.

Hearing her voice caused me to shift my focus away from the monitor. Standing there studying her, she seemed incomplete, half-dressed, and out of place. Something was clearly missing. She really needed to get those glasses.

"In your car?" I asked, still trying not to focus on her face.

She nodded her head as she brushed her dishwater blonde hair over her shoulder.

I shrugged as I turned toward my work station. "You should probably get 'em so you can see what I'm doing."

It was ten o'clock in the morning on a Wednesday, not typically a time of day when we were swamped with clients. I had owned the shop for two years, and even though business was slowly on the increase, we were far from steady with customers early in the morning on a Wednesday.

"Yeah, go get your glasses. Grab a little plaid skirt and a fucking lollipop while you're out there," Tyler said sarcastically as he continued to mess with one of his tattoo machines.

Luckily, it appeared she didn't hear him.

"I'll be right back," she said as she tugged her shirt over the waist of her jeans.

I watched her every step as she walked toward the door without seeming to care if I paid attention to her or not. As she pushed the door open, she glanced over her shoulder. I attempted unsuccessfully to seem uninterested.

"Dude..." Tyler said as the door closed behind her.

I turned toward him and grinned, well aware of where his comments were going to be directed.

"Who is she again?" I asked as I sauntered toward my work station.

"Friend of a friend." He paused, turned his stool half way around, and continued to taunt me over his shoulder.

"I wonder if she's got the skirt and the lollipop in her car. That's a bad little bitch, Blake. Be pretty tough to fight the urge to get in her pants, huh?" he said.

"Stop it. Friend of a friend, huh? Be a little more specific?" I asked as I pulled the drawer of my box open.

He shook his head. "Not really."

I looked up from the collection of tattoo machines and glanced over my left shoulder. Tyler was my first employee, and had quickly become the brother I never had growing up. He was in his late twenties, obtained half of an engineering degree at the local college, and dropped out primarily because he was bored. A few months later, he began serving an apprenticeship under another local tattoo artist, and became licensed immediately prior to me opening my shop. As soon as the lights were on and the door was open, he offered his services along with paying a healthy booth rent, stating the shop he was working for was a drama-filled distraction to his otherwise simple way of living life. In my shop, from what he shared with me, he was able to relax and enjoy being an artist.

"What the...you're seriously not going to tell me who she is or where she came from?"

"Listen. It's simple, but complicated. You know those deals where sometimes it's best just to keep your mouth shut? Well, this is one of those deals. And, you'll get her name when you make a copy of her ID. Don't forget that, you simple minded fuck. And you're trying to quit, anyway," he said.

"Huh?"

He narrowed his gaze and stared. "You're trying to quit fucking the customers, remember?"

I glanced toward the door. "Tell me, but make it quick, she'll be back in a minute."

"Not gonna happen, bro," he said as he turned away.

"Jesus, Tyler…"

"You said you're going to stop fucking the chicks that come in here. I'm just trying to help you out, bro," he said flatly as he continued to fuck with the tattoo machine he held in his hand.

"Listen, fucker. You need to tell me whatever you…"

The sound of the buzzer from the front door caused me to look away and warned me to stop talking. All recollections of Mrs. Reisling soon faded as Riley whoever she was walked into the shop wearing the biggest, boldest, hottest pair of old school frames I had ever seen. I swallowed heavily and patted the cushion of the seat in front of me.

"Grab a seat right here," I said as I slapped the leather surface with the palm of my hand.

She now looked five years older and ten times more attractive. I realized a good portion - if not all - of my attraction to women in glasses was a result of an unfulfilled childhood fantasy of boning my large-breasted glasses-donning school teacher, but it didn't matter. At that moment Riley was causing me to all but forget my entire eighth grade year of middle school.

"So, you said you've done quite a few like this?" she asked as she sat down.

I nodded my head as I reached for my book of fonts. "Yeah, quite a few."

"How many?" she asked.

"Two fucking hundred," Tyler respond over his shoulder.

"I don't know an exact amount, but it's probably over a hundred," I said as I opened the book.

Tyler glanced toward us and shook his head in apparent disgust.

I glared at him and shook my head. The last thing I needed was him trying to talk her out of getting the tattoo and having her leave before I got a chance to know more about her. I shifted my eyes toward Riley, and as she studied the book of fonts, I studied her.

Beautiful. If I had to describe her in one word, there wasn't another word that would do her justice. I had always perceived using *beautiful* as a description to be lame and cheap, but to describe Riley as anything but beautiful wouldn't give her credit where the credit was due. Sitting and gazing down at the pages of the book, she defined beauty in more ways than I could have sat and counted.

Unconsciously, and almost as if she had no idea I was at her side, she reached for the hair which hung down beside her face - partially obstructing her view of me - and brushed it behind her ear. After turning another page, she tilted her head to the side, grinned, and shifted her eyes to the pages of the book again.

"Every fucking high school girl up at East High has come in here for one of those as soon as she's eighteen. Get something original, Jesus," Tyler mumbled as he spun his stool around.

I shook my head at his off-hand remarks, relieved that Riley was paying no attention to him.

Tyler wasn't afraid to speak his mind, and if anything, he was a little too eager to do so at times. Often his remarks toward women in the shop got me into trouble. It seemed he was always trying to push me beyond a limit I was comfortable with, coercing me to do something I would normally shy away from if he was away from the shop. Recently, after much pleading for him to do so, he had begun to act as my conscience, and was attempting to assist me in my recovery from screwing the patrons.

I glanced at Riley, attempted to see beyond her glasses, and shrugged.

"It seems like every high school girl up at East High has been in here to get one of those as soon as she's eighteen. It's almost like an epidemic," I said.

She inhaled a slow breath and breathed her response. "Are you serious?"

I glanced beyond her and toward Tyler, who was behind her and well out of her field of vision. He widened his eyes, shrugged his shoulders, and gave another snide remark.

"Put some little black birds flying out of the last letter, and have 'em flying up her back and onto her fucking neck, that'd be original. What a stupid bitch," he mumbled.

I glared at him until he turned around.

"Yeah, it's a pretty common piece," I said.

She shook her head, swept the loose hair over her shoulders, and shifted her eyes to meet mine. "I don't want what everyone else has."

My gaze shifted slowly from her face to her feet, taking every inch of her in along the way. Her figure, no differently than her face, defined perfection.

"Well? What do you want to do?" I shrugged as I focused on her shoes.

"Seriously, have you done a hundred of these? Like this exact phrase?" she asked.

I shifted my eyes upward and nodded my head. "Yeah, probably."

She shook her head and handed me the book. "I don't want it, then."

Tyler raised his hands over his head and began to clap. I tossed the book of fonts to the side and reached for the neck of her shirt, attempting the entire time not to stare at her glasses.

"Get a jalapeno pepper wearing sunglasses. It's the free tattoo of the week," Tyler said over his shoulder.

"We're all about originality at my shop. It's kind of what tattoos are about. You know, expressing yourself. Would you consider yourself to be a common person?" I asked.

She shook her head. "No."

"Don't get something so common. Get something original," I said.

"Like?" she asked.

"Go big or go bigger," Tyler shouted.

I shook my head, frustrated that he wouldn't stop making snide remarks.

Tyler stood and walked toward my work station. As he twisted a rubber band around the needle of his tattoo machine, he stood behind us and studied Riley. After a long moment, he turned to face me and shrugged.

"What's her story?" he whispered.

I shrugged my shoulders and leaned toward Riley.

"What's your story?" I asked.

"What do you mean?" she responded.

"Well…" I paused, not certain of how to proceed.

Tyler stood behind her with his arms crossed, studying her. After a moment, he turned away and shook his head in frustration.

"Simple question. What's your fucking story? Everybody's got

19

one. You know, why you here? Why'd you decide all of a sudden to get a tattoo? Someone die? Have a kid? Break up with some dick? Meet someone and fall in love? Have a fucking epiphany last night at midnight? It's got to be something," Tyler mumbled as he walked away.

I waved my hand in his direction, all but forcing him to go to the other side of the shop and hopefully be quiet.

"You know, your story. What brought you here? Why'd you decide all of a sudden to get a tattoo? Did someone close to you die? Did you have a kid? Did you just end a shitty relationship, you know, break up with some dick? Did you meet someone and fall in love?" I asked.

"The third one. Broke up with some dick," she said.

I really didn't need the temptation. I almost wished she would have said she had met someone and fallen in love. It was difficult enough for me to fight my addictions of picking up a bottle of beer, having a drink, or smoking a joint with Tyler. Above all, my addiction to women was the worst, and Riley was easily the best looking specimen I had seen in a long, long time.

Knowing she was single made matters much worse.

"Talk her into getting a koi fish or a fucking snake. A koi depicts courage, and a snake represents rebirth, a transformation, and healing. Get a fucking snake *and* a koi," Tyler said.

"What do you think of a koi fish or a snake or something? They're representations of courage, rebirth, healing…"

She clasped her hands together as if she were cold, and squeezed her biceps against rather nicely shaped breasts. "You think that's better than the Latin?"

She looked innocent, young, and gorgeous. It was quite possible my six weeks of abstaining from sex had hindered my vision slightly, but in anyone's eyes, Riley would have been beyond what one could describe as attractive. In my eyes, she was quickly becoming a person I was incapable of walking away from. The more I looked at her, the less faults I found. In five more minutes, she'd be perfect.

I needed to quit admiring her before something bad happened.

Tyler's eyes widened comically. "Are you fucking serious? Having a snake tattooed on you says "I'm a bad ass". But tattooing a statement on you that says "Hey, I'm a bad ass" says you're nothing but a douchebag. Getting that Latin phrase, in my opinion, is fucking stupid. Get something that *symbolizes* your thoughts and feelings. Or, I guess Blake could tattoo something on your back that says 'I met a guy and fell in love, we broke up, now I feel strong and empowered, and I think I'm headed down the path of living a new courageous life,' and he could do it in Greek or Spanish or some shit."

Riley sat and gazed at me as if waiting on direction.

"Well, I believe saying something with words is the easy way out. What if Leonardo da Vinci would have written a paragraph depicting his thoughts instead of painting the Mona Lisa? Can you imagine that? I think a picture is worth a thousand words," I said.

"Well, I'll trust your judgement. I just don't want to be like everyone else," she said.

"I've got a bad ass koi already drawn up over here," I said as I reached toward my cabinet.

After rifling through the many drawings on top of my cabinet, I produced the koi fish. I flattened the paper and held it in the air for her to see.

"I like it. What color would you do?" she asked as she studied the drawing.

"Orange on the fish. It's pretty traditional. It stands for good fortune. We could surround it with blues, pinks, or purples. It'd really pop."

"Sounds great. Let's do that," she responded. "I really don't want something a bunch of other girls have tattooed on them."

"It's going to be a little more expensive than the phrase," I said.

She shrugged her shoulders. "It doesn't matter. I'll pay whatever it costs."

"That's what I like to hear," I said.

"Problem fucking solved," Tyler said.

"So, you want to go with this?" I asked as I stood from my seat.

She nodded her head and grinned.

"Let me make a stencil and we'll get started. It's going to take about six hours, so probably two three-hour sessions. Is that alright?" I asked. "Oh, and I'll need to make a copy of your ID. And I'll have a form for you to sign."

"Okay," she said as she reached for her purse. "Here."

I glanced down at her driver's license as I walked away. Riley J. Campbell, D.O.B. September 24, 1993. She wasn't even twenty-two yet, and looked every bit of twenty-five or twenty-six.

"You haven't got time to finish it today?" she asked as I walked away.

I turned around as I shrugged my shoulders. "I've got time, but it'll be pretty painful to sit there and get pounded on for six hours."

"Six hours of that needle will be a lot better than the poundings I'm used to," she responded.

"We'll try and finish it today then," I said as I turned toward the copy machine.

Tyler's secrecy regarding who she was and her comment about

being pounded on raised my level of interest in her considerably. If I didn't offer to exchange a tattoo for sex, and instead spent the next six hours trying to get to know her, in my mind I'd still be recovering from my addictions and not succumbing to temptation.

In theory, it sounded good.

I knew all she would really need to do to cause me to grovel at her feet would be to have her hair in a ponytail. Something about a girl with a strong jawline and a ponytail always appealed to me. Riley had a great jaw, high cheeks, and when combined with her glasses, a ponytail would without a doubt put me over the edge.

After making a copy of the drawing and her license, I turned to face her.

"Hope you're ready," I said as I raised the stencil in the air.

She reached for her wrist and then over her shoulders with both hands.

"I'll just get this mop out of your way," she said as she twisted her hair into a ponytail, "And then you can get to work."

I did my best to look beyond her. As my eyes came into focus along the far wall, Tyler held both fists to his side and extended his thumbs upward. As his mouth curled into a huge grin he nodded his head in Riley's direction.

Damn you, Tyler, stop it.

I shifted my focus to her. She glanced upward, grinned, and peered through her bold black fuck-me frames, knowing nothing of what she was doing to me.

Or, maybe she knew everything of what she was doing to me.

I returned her gaze, smiled, and sat down. As I spun my stool away from her and grabbed a pair of rubber gloves, I closed my eyes.

BLURRED LINES

God, grant me the serenity to accept the things I cannot change; the courage to change the things I can; and the wisdom to know the difference.

I opened my eyes, pulled the gloves over my sweaty hands, and turned to face her.

Sitting in the chair smiling, her hair pulled back into a ponytail and her black glasses perched high on her nose, she stared innocently in my direction.

They told me the program for recovery was simple.

They lied.

RILEY

I expected the process to be painful, but the pain I felt during the procedure was more of a hypnotic feeling, something I not only quickly became used to, but actually had developed a fondness for. My glances over my shoulder and into the mirror, the amount of time that had passed, and Blake's updates let me know he was close to being finished; something I really wasn't prepared for.

I wanted him to continue. The sharp needle caused a dull predictable pain - something I felt much deeper than my skin. It seemed to be pounding into my very soul. Although I couldn't speak for anyone else, it became apparent why so many people were covered with tattoos. The feeling, in itself, was addictive.

I realized as sure as I was sitting there having him grind the needle into my flesh that not only was this my first tattoo, but it was far from the last I would ever receive. The five and a half hours which had passed had done so rather quickly, and as I considered having him continue with another tattoo on my opposite shoulder, the buzzing stopped as he dipped the needle into the ink again.

"You're a fucking trooper," he said as the machine began to buzz again.

Craning my neck over my shoulder and watching him focus on his work was interesting. Although I realized it was necessary for him to study his work and maintain focus, his intensity was apparent. With his jaw clenched, his eyes narrowed slightly, and the muscles in his forearm flexed, he gazed past the buzzing machine and focused on the tip of the needle almost as if he was looking beyond where it made contact with my skin. At times, I felt as if he was peering into my very soul.

And his eyes.

His eyes were an unidentifiable color. At times they appeared to be as green as translucent grass. Moments later, they were a glowing bronze. But they were always mysterious.

"What do you mean?" I asked as I pried my eyes away from him.

"Been sitting here for six fucking hours letting me drill on ya without saying a word, that's what I mean. Most people would have thrown in the towel. You're a trooper. Looks pretty damned good, too," he said.

I nodded my head and bit my lip as he continued to work toward completion. Another song I didn't recognize filled the room. I wondered if the music he had playing was some special tattoo music that outsiders weren't able to hear otherwise.

"Who's this?" I asked as the woman's voice softly sang of solitude.

"Who's what?" he asked over the buzzing of the tattoo machine.

"The music, who is this?" I asked.

"Oh, this?"

The buzzing stopped momentarily, and I heard him sigh. After a short pause, the buzzing continued and he pressed the needle into my skin again.

"Del Bel. Name of the song is *In My Solitude*," he said.

I nodded my head lightly. "I like it."

Losing myself in the next two or three songs was easy. The music seemed to sooth me and slowly took my mind well beyond the oddly comforting pain. After what seemed like a matter of minutes, his speaking broke the silence.

"About fifteen minutes," he said as he paused to dip the needle in the ink well again.

I wet my lips and peered over my shoulder. "Have time to get started on the snake?"

"Not today. Six hours is about the limit. You'll go into shock if we continue," he responded.

"I'm good," I said.

"You might think you are, but you're not," he said.

"No really…"

"We can make an appointment for this weekend, or here in a few days, but not today, believe me, you'll need to recover from this," he said.

I really wanted the tattoo, but I hoped to come back and see him even more so. I realized he knew more about the process than I, and responded reluctantly.

"Okay."

During the final minutes of the tattoo, I somehow found a peaceful place for my mind to reside. Visions of a new me - one who was carefree, living an uncomplicated life free to make choices filled my mind. Within what seemed like a matter of minutes, the dull drone of the machine stopped.

Blake lifted the needle from my skin.

"I'm going to wipe this, it'll be tender," he said.

"Okay," I responded.

As he wiped across the freshly tattooed area, I winced. The predictable pain from the needle piercing my skin turned to a dull throb covering my entire right shoulder. Again he wiped the cold paper towel across my shoulder, causing me to close my eyes and shrug my shoulders from the pain.

"Take a look at that," he said as he slid his stool in front of me.

I stood from my seat and immediately felt lightheaded. Blake was right, although I was mentally eager to continue with another tattoo, I was far from being physically ready for another session. I walked to the mirror, turned around, and pulled the neck of my shirt down.

My shoulder was swollen, but the detail, color, and quality of his artistry were apparent. The orange koi was highlighted with a few white and black specs, surrounded with blue water, deeper blue and waves that faded into purple, and the entire tattooed area was speckled with a few pink cherry blossoms. As a symbol of my rebirth or simply as a tattoo of an orange fish, it was beautiful.

"I love it. Can I uhhm. Can I take off my shirt? I have a sports bra on. I mean, people jog in them and stuff," I said as I continued to admire the tattoo in the mirror.

"Sure. Let me help you," he responded.

He stood from his seat, removed his gloves, and stepped in front of me. As he reached for the waist of my shirt, he nodded his head toward the other side of the shop.

"Grab the back of her shirt and help me out," he said.

I reached down and grabbed the waist of my shirt.

Blake shook his head. "No, *you* stand still. You stretch that tattoo out and it'll be painful. Sorry, I was thinking Tyler was still here, but he must have slipped out. I'll get it."

He turned his head to the side and leaned forward, almost touching his chest to mine. As he shifted his hands to the sides of my shirt, he lifted carefully, pulling it rearward, and away from the tattoo. I closed my eyes and inhaled a shallow breath through my nose, hoping to catch a hint of something memorable about his scent. All I got was a faint smell of my own perfume.

"Raise your arms," he said.

Once again, his breath against my neck caused goosebumps to rise along my upper arms. As I felt the shirt being pulled over my head, I opened my eyes and turned toward the mirror.

"Much better," I said.

"I agree," he responded.

"Excuse me?" I asked.

He shrugged his shoulders as he hung my shirt over the back of the chair I had been sitting in. "I didn't say anything."

After stretching plastic wrap over the tattooed area, taping it into place, and going over the required aftercare with me, I realized it was time for me to pay for the tattoo and leave. I didn't mind paying, but the leaving wasn't something I was really prepared to do, at least not just yet.

"How much do I owe you?" I asked.

"Six hours at one-thirty an hour would normally be seven-eighty. Let's call it six hundred," he responded.

"Are tips customary?" I asked.

"If you're pleased."

I was pleased. Even though I realized he needed to concentrate on his work, I did talk to him quite a bit during the beginning of the session. He reluctantly responded to each question, offering quick explanations to my tattoo related ignorance, and was rather polite throughout the entire procedure.

The last few hours of the tattoo had been rather quiet, my having obviously fallen into a state of semi-hypnosis attributing to at least a portion of my silence. I did, however, learn a little about Blake during the first few hours.

He was single, he owned the tattoo shop, and he rode a motorcycle even when it was raining outside.

In short, I was interested in knowing much more about him.

"Here's my card for the six hundred, and here's two hundred for a tip," I said as I handed him two one hundred dollar bills and my debit card.

"Damn, you sure?" he asked as he accepted the money.

I shifted my eyes from my hand to his face. His narrow eyes, the short growth of beard, and his heavily tattooed body was more than tempting. The way his shirt now hung from his perfectly defined chest was too much. I glanced down at his feet.

Old school Vans.

Cute.

As he walked away I glanced in his direction. A perfectly round man ass was hiding beneath his jeans. In admiration of his discipline, I nodded my head. Most men chose to work out their arms and chest and neglected the legs and butt. It was pretty obvious he wasn't one of those men, and as I filled my eyes with the backside of his faded jeans, I was grateful.

"I'm very happy with it. And I'm glad you didn't let me get the other one," I said.

"I'm glad you didn't get it," he said over his shoulder.

I slowly walked in his direction, admiring him the entire way.

"Make me an appointment for my other shoulder, too. While we're up here," I said.

"Snake?" he asked.

"Mmmhhhmmm," I responded.

"Saturday's full, let's see…" he said as he fumbled with the mouse and stared at the screen of his computer.

"Tomorrow?" I asked.

He tilted his head to the side. "You off work tomorrow?"

"Yeah."

"How about Friday? That'll give you a day to recover. We can at least do the outline and see how you feel."

"Okay," I said.

"Same time?" he asked as he rubbed his hands together.

Something I was sure he didn't even realize he did, but was somewhat of a nervous tick, his rubbing his hands together was enjoyable to watch. He did it with such ferocity; it was almost as if he was attempting to start a fire. And, as he did it, the muscles on his upper arms and chest flared, making the entire process even more enjoyable to me. As I studied his chest and admired the tattoo of a dragon which covered his forearm, the credit card machine spit out my receipt.

As he reached for the receipt, a pin-up girl on his bicep crept from underneath the sleeve of his tee shirt. I wondered as he glanced down at the piece of paper just what he had tattooed on the parts of his body that weren't exposed. Some things, I guessed, were best left to the imagination.

I shrugged my shoulders as he handed me the card and my receipt. I considered the benefits of having the tattoo last until closing time, and potentially finishing it late or after hours. If nothing else, maybe we could sit and talk, getting to know each other a little bit more. It was nice to talk to someone and not have them constantly forcing themselves upon me or beating the shit out of me later.

The fact he was smoking hot made being in his presence that much more enjoyable.

"Same time really doesn't work. I forgot, I've got a lunch date with a girlfriend on Friday," I lied.

He twisted his mouth to the side and stared at the monitor.

"When do you close?" I asked.

"Nine," he said.

Assuming the snake tattoo would take the same amount of time as the koi, I counted backward from the time he closed.

"How's three o'clock sound? Three or four?" I asked.

He glanced at the computer screen.

"Sounds good," he shrugged.

"Let's make it four. Just to be safe," I said.

"Done," he said as he leaned away from the monitor.

I signed the receipt and handed it to him. "Thank you, I love it."

"You look good as fuck," he said.

"Excuse me?" I asked.

"Your tattoo looks good as fuck," he said as he turned away.

"See you Friday," he said.

I nodded my head and turned away.

I wanted more. Maybe all tattoo artists were slightly pretentious and kind of skittish. I had no idea and no experience to make comparisons. As I made my way toward the door, I realized my shoulder was in severe pain, and it was only a little after three in the afternoon.

As I stepped through the door, I glanced over my shoulder and into the shop. Blake stood in front of his work area rubbing his hands together and talking to himself. I paused, watched him for a moment, and became even more intrigued by his oddly interesting nature. Eventually I turned toward the car, realized it was half a mile away, and wished I had parked a little bit closer.

As the afternoon sun beat down on my bare stomach, I realized I was walking down the street in my bra. And, although I hadn't intended to do so, I left my shirt draped over the back of Blake's chair.

I considered going back to get it for about half a second. If nothing else, it would give me a reason to go and see him the next day.

And that was exactly what I intended to do.

BLAKE

Trying to decide which direction to take my life wasn't easy, but I had finally reached a point where it was necessary. Three stints in jail for driving under the influence of alcohol, losing my license for almost a decade, and dealing drugs to pay my legal fees weren't the best decisions I ever made, but they were part of who I was, regardless. In being honest, they were all the proof I needed to convince myself I had a problem that needed to be addressed, but addressing it was still difficult.

Finally, an intervention of sorts convinced me.

More like a revelation.

Or an awakening.

Whatever it was, the cab fare associated with it was expensive, and I viewed the event, in its entirety, as the last straw.

I had somehow ended up in a bathtub in someone's home I didn't know. I had no recollection of going there, or even considering it, but nonetheless, I was there, naked, and confused. I came out of my unconscious state of being blacked out - something I normally did after a few dozen drinks - and looked around the bathroom. Covered in soap suds and as naked as the day I was born, I was shocked, scared, and for some reason, sexually aroused beyond compare.

As I sat in the warm tub with a raging hard on, trying to figure out how I got there and what I was doing, an unfamiliar voice from the other room caused me to wonder even more. I should have been relieved that I was in a stranger's tub and a woman was involved, but I wasn't.

After all, matters could have been much worse.

She walked into the bathroom carrying two flutes of champagne, humming an unfamiliar and rather annoying off-key tune. I glanced over the edge of the tub and around the bathroom, hoping to catch a glimpse of where I had dropped my clothes, but the room was void of any of my attire.

Frustrated with myself, disgusted with her, and ready to leave, I stood from the tub and grabbed one of the flutes of champagne. After downing it in one gulp, I proudly walked past her, placed the empty glass on the vanity, and stepped into the adjoining room.

Nothing.

"Where are you going?" she asked.

I gazed out the window and into the driveway.

My bike wasn't anywhere to be found, and the neighborhood didn't look at all familiar.

With no clothes, no cellphone, no bike, and no recollection of where I had been prior to arriving in the tub, I sat naked on her couch and searched my mind for even the vaguest of answers.

And I drew a blank.

"Where am I?" I asked as she walked into the room.

I was barely thirty. She appeared to be in her mid-sixties.

And she was still naked.

"What do you mean?" she asked.

"I must have blacked out. What happened? Where am I?" I asked as I looked around the room.

"Well, you left the bar with me, we came here, and we ended up in the tub. After a while I decided to get us some champagne. You said it sounded like a good idea. You don't remember any of it?" she asked.

I shook my head. I didn't even want to know why my cock was hard or what transpired between our having arrived in the tub and "after a while." Completely disgusted with her, my drunken behavior, and the fact I still had no idea of what city I was in, I took inventory of the room one more time in hopes of seeing my jeans, phone, wallet, or shoes.

"Are we in Wichita?" I asked after my search produced nothing.

"Hutchinson. You really don't remember?"

Hutchison was sixty miles from my home, and not a place I had ever been short of one drunken trip to the state fair to see lobster boy and the man with snake scales for skin.

I shook my head. "Where are my clothes?"

"In my bedroom? You don't remember that either?"

"I don't remember anything. Can you point me in that direction?" I asked.

After getting dressed, finding my wallet, phone, and shoes, I called a cab. I told the cab driver after paying a $300 fare that I was never going to take another drink.

And I had yet to break my promise.

"Hi, my name's Blake, and I'm addicted to everything," I said.

"Hi Blake," a handful of people said in response.

"What is sobriety? Was that it? The topic?" I asked.

Several people nodded their heads.

I nodded mine in confirmation and began speaking.

"Well, I think it's much more than abstaining from taking the first drink. It's a state of mind as well. Sobriety, at least to me, is the art of being sober, not the act. I think it comes over the course of time, roughly at the time when we become comfortable that what it is we're doing is exactly what we should be doing when we should be doing it. In the beginning I was abstaining, and as a matter of definition I suppose I was sober, but I wasn't living a life of sobriety. I was a drunken idiot without a bottle in my hand. "

I paused and thought for a moment.

"Now, I really think I am sober. But, to be honest, I'm a sober idiot. You know, I hoped sobering up would cause me to make more intelligent decisions, but it didn't. Now, I'm sober, but I'm still a fucking idiot. Blake the sober idiot since September 11th. Tell me that isn't fucking ironic, huh? A sobriety date of nine-eleven. Well, at least I'll never forget it. And, like I said, I'm addicted to everything, so I'm struggling with trying not to bone this gorgeous chick that came in for a tattoo the other day. For right now, I'm pretty sure I'll keep away from my first drink, but I'm not making any promises about staying out of her pants. That's all I've got," I said.

"Thanks Blake, glad you're here," a woman from across the table said.

I nodded my head in her direction.

She stared.

I glanced away from her, stood, and walked to the coffee bar. As I turned away from the pot, I almost ran into her.

"Oh shit. Sorry, I didn't even see you," I said.

"I was sneaking up on you," she said.

"Well, you did a good job," I said as I attempted to step around her.

"So, want to get a cup of coffee after the meeting?" she asked as she stepped to the side.

She was in her early forties and attractive in her own way, but not someone I would ever be interested in. Although she was probably someone I needed to be hanging out with, and also a person I could spend plenty of time with without trying to fuck her, I shook my head.

"Sorry, I've got to get back to work," I responded.

"Well, anytime you want to, just say the word," she said.

"Bet on it," I said as I stepped past her.

Truth be known, I'd sign up for a keg stand contest before I'd have a cup of coffee with her.

If I was going to be talking to anyone, it was going to be Riley, and for some damned reason getting her off of my mind was proving to be impossible. I'd only done one tattoo on her, and in the grand scheme of things, it was nothing. I'd done three times as many on hundreds of women without thinking about them after they had walked out of the shop.

Riley seemed to be searching for something, but I had my doubts she even knew what it was she was trying to find. I glanced at my watch. Less than twenty-four hours and I'd see her again.

If Tyler wasn't going to tell me anything about her, I intended to press her hard for answers during her next session. Not fucking her was the key to maintaining my peace of mind, but that didn't mean I couldn't get to know her.

I sat in my seat and sipped my cup of coffee while some old timer explained what sobriety meant to him. As I listened to him talk, but make absolutely no sense whatsoever, I wished I could live a normal life.

But anyone who survived what I had survived would never live a normal life.

I simply needed to find a way to accept my parent's death as being something completely out of reach for me to resolve.

    Doing so, however, was a different story.

RILEY

I parked my car in the same spot, checked myself in the mirror, and glanced down at my bare legs. At the time it seemed like a great idea, but now that I was sitting in my car down the street from the tattoo shop in my neon pink boy shorts and sports bra, I felt like a slightly arrogant slut.

I was better than this.

Much better.

I convinced myself it was alright to stop by because I had been at the YMCA, and the gym was in the neighborhood. In my way of thinking, it was alright to stop and pick up my shirt from Blake; in fact, it just made good sense to do it while I was in the neighborhood. Realistically, I could have easily picked it up when I came in four hours later for him to do my tattoo.

As I fought with myself regarding what I should do, a figure in the distance caught my attention. Blake stood outside the tattoo shop, leaning against the wall smoking a cigarette.

Shit.

If I drove away, I'd have to drive past him, and would risk him seeing me and wondering why I was doing a drive by. And, if I got out and walked his direction, I would risk him thinking I was a dumb underdressed slut with a high sex drive. As I told myself never to fall victim to my mindless ways of thinking again, he leaned forward and peered down the block and through the windshield.

His eyesight must be much better than mine.

Within a few seconds, he was waving his arm as if to guide me in. I shifted the car into gear and slowly rolled his direction. As the car pulled in front of the shop, I parked and reluctantly opened the door.

"I just got done working out, and was thinking about stopping and getting my shirt. Then I realized I was in workout gear, and I thought maybe I'd just wait. Gonna be in here in a few hours anyway," I said over the top of the car.

"Nice car, it's on my bucket list," he said as he flicked his cigarette into the street.

A few dozen cigarette butts slightly beyond the curb acted as camouflage to the new addition.

"It's fun to drive," I said as I shifted my eyes from the pile of cigarette butts.

"Zero to sixty in less than four seconds is more than fun. *Exhilarating* is what *Road and Track* said when they tested it," he said.

"You know your cars," I said.

"I know a little bit about a lot of things. Come on in, we're not prejudiced about clothing," he said as he turned toward the door.

I inhaled a shallow breath of courage, exhaled, and began walking toward the shop as soon as he was through the door. As I approached the entrance, I felt naked and exposed. I never realized what it was about working out, but I rarely felt uncomfortable in boy shorts and a sports bra while I was at the gym, but being anywhere else in public with the same attire caused me to feel naked.

Being with Stephen from the time I was seventeen until I was twenty-one left me with very little experience in communicating or interacting with men. I wasn't a fool by any means, but walking through the door of Blake's shop with my ass cheeks hanging out of my shorts, I sure felt like one.

"Here you go," he said as he turned around.

He held my shirt in front of his chest with both hands. Neatly folded, it appeared that he may have washed it.

"You didn't wash it did you?" I asked.

He nodded his head. "Sure did."

"Wow, thanks," I said as I reached for the shirt.

I carefully held the shirt no differently than he did, being cautious not to wrinkle it.

"Turn around, let me have a look at that new piece," he said.

"It's doing really good. Got a few comments at the gym. I don't know how long it usually takes, but it doesn't hurt anymore. I think it's healed."

"It's far from healed," he said with a laugh. "Turn around."

I turned around and faced the entrance as he stepped behind me. Although it had only been two days, the tattoo was no longer painful, and seemed to be more colorful than the day he did the work.

His presence behind me caused me to feel nervous and as if I was in high school again, feeling nervously sick when I was near a boy I felt affectionate about. He lifted my ponytail, held it in his hand, and mumbled to himself as he inspected the tattoo. I stood holding the shirt in my hands, waiting for him to critique my tattoo maintenance procedures. I lowered my head, peered down at my oversized feet, and wished I had worn my other shoes.

"Just keep it lubricated," he breathed against the back of my neck.

My knees all but buckled as I inhaled sharply.

"Is it okay?" I asked as I turned around.

"Looks fucking awesome," he responded.

He stood in front of me in similar tattered tee shirt to what he was wearing when I met him, rubbing his hands together frantically. The outline of the large cross that hung in the center of his chest was well-defined as the shirt he was wearing fit him all too well. His nervous nature was cute, and I wondered what went through his mind while he was rubbing his palms together, if anything. I believed there was far more to Blake the tattoo artist than what I was seeing, and I wanted to take as much time as necessary to find out everything I could about him.

"So, not too busy today?" I asked as I looked around the empty shop.

"No, Tyler went to get us a sandwich or something. I just got done with my second little piece. You're my next appointment," he responded. "Want to just get started now?"

My previous notions regarding tattooed men was that they were all former military, bikers, or sailors my father's age or older. I never really considered a man covered in tattoos to be "normal" looking or attractive. Blake was both. His body was attractive, tattooed or not, and his face was handsome yet slightly boyish. His hair was a perfect mess, much longer on top than the sides - and had just the right amount of product in it, assuring that it was always the same amount of messed up.

In my mind, he was perfect, or at least he appeared to be on the surface.

I really would have rather stayed, but staying would have meant he would be done with my tattoo at about six o'clock, not at closing time. I really hoped to be there when he closed, and maybe he'd invite me to stay and talk. I had no real intention of doing anything more, and getting to know him would be nice.

No doubt a luxury I had yet to enjoy.

I found it quite sad that I was twenty-one years old, and really hadn't spent any time talking to or getting to know another man. Since my junior year in high school, the only man I ever spoke to was Stephen. It was no wonder I wore my boy shorts to try and entice Blake to talk to me.

"No, I need to get home and take a shower. I'll probably be right on time, four o'clock, right?" I asked, knowing full well what time the appointment was.

"Yep, four. Well," he paused and glanced down at my feet.

He slowly shifted his gaze up and along my body, and grinned when his eyes met mine. Feeling like I was being peeked at through a hole in the girls shower room, I nervously pulled my shirt to my chest and attempted to cover myself as best as I was able.

"What?" I breathed.

"Damn shame Tyler isn't here, he'd have something to say about that outfit," he said.

"Think so?" I asked.

"Know so. That fucking Tyler, he loves boy shorts. Those are boy shorts, right? That's what you call 'em?" he asked as he tilted his head downward.

Slightly embarrassed, but not so much that I felt uncomfortable, I widened my eyes and grinned.

"Yeah, that's what they call 'em," I responded.

"Well, he'll be back here in a few, you probably better sneak out while you can. I need to get this shit cleaned up before he gets back here with lunch. Guess I'll see you here in a bit," he said.

"Okay," I said as I turned away, feeling as if I was being ushered out, "I'll see you at four."

He followed me to the door, walked outside with me, and leaned against the brick wall as I walked away. Half way to my car, I peered over my shoulder and waved. He stood beside the entrance with his feet crossed, smoking a cigarette.

Leaning against the building smoking, he could have easily been posing for the cover of a magazine. His hair had fallen into his eyes slightly, and his cigarettes were rolled into the left sleeve of his shirt. With his faded boot-cut jeans and worn sneakers, a cloud of smoke rose from his mouth and disappeared into the air. In a black and white photo, he could have passed for an actor from a movie scene out of the 1950's.

I unlocked my car, opened the passenger door, and carefully placed the folded shirt on the seat. After shutting the door and checking traffic, I walked around the back of the car and opened the driver's door. Standing with the edge of the door cradled in my hand, I gazed up the sidewalk and toward the shop.

He appeared to be either singing a song or talking to himself. His mouth was moving, and his hands were busy motioning toward the street. One more puff from his cigarette, and he flicked it into the street amongst the others littering the curb in front of his shop. After exhaling his smoke into the air, he turned away and disappeared into the shop.

Blake was an interesting man. In four more hours, I was going to try and find out as much about him as he would let me.

I just needed to decide how much regarding my own life I was going to be willing to part with to lure him in.

BLAKE

My life was filled with distractions. My addictions, at least by my own self-diagnosis, were all a result of me attempting to rid myself of the things that lingered in my mind. Never an easy task, the objects and events of my past seemed to not only overtake my thoughts, but become part of who I was.

I had always felt a joint or a drink was the best way to minimize my recurring thoughts and clear my mind. Now, even though I could declare sobriety as being something I had obtained, the distractions continued, but were in a different form.

"Listen, I'm not going to have you here fucking with me the entire time I'm trying to tattoo her. I promise, I'm not going to try and fuck her tonight. Hell, maybe never, I don't know. But tonight? It's not going to happen," I said as I pilfered through my drawer full of tattoo machines.

"Gorgeous bitch like that? Dude, she'll be sucking your cock as soon as you're done with the shoulder piece. You and I both know it. She made that late appointment for a reason, she wants you," Tyler said as he stood from his stool.

I shook my head as I gazed into the drawer, eventually shifting my eyes in his direction.

"You can be a prick sometimes. I'm trying to get better. I might end up wanting to do something with her, but it's going to be a long time,

47

and I'm gonna to do it right. Seriously, I'm getting better," I tried to assure him.

"Lemme ask you a question," he said.

"Ask away," I responded.

"When she came in earlier, was she wearing her glasses?" he asked.

I nodded my head as I pulled the machine with the knurled brass grip from the drawer.

"Fuck yes, I knew this was in here," I said as I admired the machine.

"Answer the question, Blake," he said.

"Glasses? Yeah, she can't see without them," I responded.

"Whatever. Did she have her hair in a fucking ponytail?" he asked.

"Yeah, she had a ponytail, she'd been at the gym."

"You're a fucking blind idiot," he huffed. "Tell me this, what was she wearing?"

I stood from my seat and placed the tattoo machine on the bench beside my box.

"Listen. She's not what you think."

"Oh really? Okay, tell me what you know about her, Detective," he said as he crossed his arms in front of his chest.

"I know her name and her birthday. I know she seems a little nervous around me, and that's a good sign. I know that she seems genuinely interested, and this isn't the typical client-aritst..."

"You don't know shit. Who wouldn't seem nervous around you, you weird fuck?" he interrupted.

"Fuck you," I snapped back.

"No dude. Fuck you. You asked for my help, and I'm trying to give it. You're justifying things. You're setting yourself up for a failure. You're going to bend that chick over and shove her full of cock. It's what you do, you can't help yourself. Let me ask you something. One more question, then I'll leave you alone," he said as he lowered his arms and walked in my direction.

"Fine."

"What was she wearing?" he asked.

"When?"

He stared down at the floor. After a long moment of appearing frustrated, he shifted his eyes upward. His gaze was one of question and concern.

"When she graduated high school, you dumb ass. Jesus. What was she wearing when she came in today? You know, when she stopped in out of the blue to get her shirt that she didn't need and she very fucking well could have got when she came in later on today. What was she wearing?" he asked.

"Sports bra, workout shoes, and some of those little shorts," I shrugged.

"Those little shorts? Jean shorts? Those big oversized swishy fuckers that the softball players wear? Cargo shorts? What kind of shorts, Blake?" he asked in a more demanding tone.

"Boy shorts," I responded.

"Boy shorts?" he laughed, "She wore boy shorts?"

I nodded my head.

"Ass cheeks hanging out and everything, right?" he chuckled.

I shrugged my shoulders, "Fuck I don't know."

"The fuck you don't. She came in here half fucking naked and got a shirt she didn't need. She's testing you, Dude. She's probably going to plop her face in your lap and swallow your rod and ask if you can do that piece while she sucks you off. Wait and see," he said as he spun around

49

and stomped toward his work station.

"She's not a skank," I said.

"Oh really? Comes in here with her ass falling out of some spandex underwear and her nipples so hard they can cut a fucking diamond, and she's not a skank. Her nipples were hard, weren't they?" he asked over his shoulder.

I was done listening to him. His efforts to keep me from acting on my addictive behavior had become more than annoying. I glanced at the clock. It was fifteen minutes until four.

"Listen," I paused, cleared my throat, and changed my tone to a harsh demanding one.

"You said you're waiting on walk-ins? Well, go home. You're done for the day," I barked as I pointed toward the door.

"Fuck that. I'm staying. Someone's got to keep your dumb ass in line," he responded.

"No. This is my shop. You're fucking done. Now, get the fuck out in the next fifteen minutes," I growled as I pointed toward the back door, "I'm going to go smoke and when I come back in here you better be gone."

He waved his hand my direction as he turned toward the door. "Fine, Asshole. I hope that little bitch brings in a sack of weed, an eight ball of coke, and a jug of fucking scotch. And I hope you fall down on her dick first. I'll be gone, don't fucking worry. I'm about done trying to help you."

I reached for my cigarettes, pulled one out, and rolled the remaining pack into my shirt sleeve. As I tapped the butt of the cigarette onto the face of my watch I walked toward the door.

"I smoke fast, so you better fucking hurry," I said as I pushed the door open.

I stepped onto the sidewalk, leaned against the wall, and lifted my shaking hand to my mouth. Tyler may have become the brother I always wanted, but since my attempt at sobriety, he was more and more protective of me with each passing day. His manner of sheltering me from myself - at least when it came to Riley - was becoming more aggressive in nature than what I was comfortable with.

The cigarette calmed my nerves and allowed me to come back down to earth. As I took my last drag and prepared to toss the butt into the street, I recognized the headlights of Riley's BMW.

I glanced at my watch.

Five minutes early.

Long before I suspected she noticed me, I flicked the cigarette aside and turned toward the shop. A precursory glance through the glass indicated Tyler had taken my advice. As I pushed the door open, the empty stool at his work station confirmed my suspicion.

I would spend the night alone.

Well, not exactly, but as close to alone as I wanted to be.

RILEY

As ridiculous as it seemed, I had spent the last four hours counting the minutes until I was going in for my new tattoo; checking my watch every fifteen minutes hoping somehow an hour had passed, only to find out it had been minutes. After changing outfits no less than six times, I finally settled for jean shorts, my tattered Chuck's, and a freshly purchased, but vintage appearing *Clash* concert tee shirt.

I had no way of knowing if my obsessive behavior was normal, or even if it would qualify as obsession for that matter, but I really didn't care. I felt like my interest in Blake was genuine, without any real motive, and harmless. After convincing myself that no one would be able to schedule when their life presented a person of interest, I dismissed my thoughts and feelings to be nothing more than reaction to a good opportunity.

I hated to call it fate, because the word made everything seem so cliché. Fate, to me, was reserved for romantic comedies, love songs, and a few well written books. Realistically speaking, there was no such thing as fate. The world spins, we stumble forward in life, and if we're paying close attention, sometimes through the course of our stumbling we bump into someone who catches our interest.

Blake surely caught mine.

I sat in my car waiting for four o'clock to arrive, wondering how much different a person I would be if I had never met Stephen. The summer after my junior year in high school we met, and immediately following, we started seeing each other. Within a year, I had graduated high school, and against the demands of my mother, I moved in with him. He was nine years older than me and had just completed law school two years prior.

At the time, his manner of dress, his many cars, and his attentive nature caused me to yearn to share my time with him. Fairly quickly, I fell in love. In hindsight, I was young, immature, and all too eager to fall for someone who provided me with an ounce of attention. My having grown up in a single parent home with a working mother and no siblings made my appetite for affection far greater than it would have been for anyone else my age.

I clung to Stephen like gum to a shoe. My plans to attend college were soon cast aside after promises that everything I wanted, desired, needed, or required would be provided to me without question as long as I was loyal to him and his needs.

So, the little girl who resided within me looked at him in a fatherly sort of way, and I fell deeply in love with what it was he provided me. Protection, comfort, love, affection, and a good hard fucking a few times a day convinced me he was nothing short of the answer to my dreams. Constantly showered with gifts, money, and clothes, it was difficult for anyone to convince me that my best interest wasn't exactly what Stephen was furnishing.

I dismissed the violent outbursts to my immature behavior, and told myself as soon as I matured fully, I would stop making the same mistakes, and the abuse would stop. In time, I did mature, yet cruel behavior continued.

I had never, however, had a chance to live life. I had no friends, not even anyone I could call an associate. All of the people I came in contact with were Stephen's friends and associates, none of which were close to my age, and in no way were any of them interested in me beyond what they expected Stephen would require of them. When we split up, there was no huge argument, no fight, and no text messages or calls following my having left.

As one of the bank accounts had both of our names on it, and was primarily used for my shopping sprees, I drove to the bank and asked about having his name removed from the account. Because we shared the account, and I was listed as the primary account holder, I removed his name without incident. I told myself it was what I was entitled to as his spouse, and although I fully expected him to make an attempt to recover the money, he never made a single effort. The state in which we resided dictated I was entitled to half of what he owned, and the portion I decided to take was more like five percent of his earnings or estate.

We had discussed a prenuptial contract on many occasions, and although I knew from his explaining matters that we were married as a matter of law, I refused to sign a prenuptial agreement, feeling it cheapened the relationship.

I suspected one of the reasons I never heard from Stephen was that I had warned him of my intention if he ever hit me again. The other reason, I was quite certain, was that when I obtained control of the account we shared, he was able to see exactly what I took, identify it, and accept is as a loss, knowing it ended there.

It was apparent he accepted it, as he chose to allow me to disappear from his life without so much as a text message.

If I were able, I would give everything back to him just to have a chance to begin my life again from scratch. If nothing else, I was grateful that I was only twenty-one years old, and had my entire remaining life ahead of me, and shared no children with him.

I glanced at my watch.

Ten after four.

Fuck.

I jumped from the car and pressed the lock button on the key fob. After making my way to the sidewalk I realized I had parked in the same spot, a hundred yards away, and with no good reason. Blake had seen what I drove, and made no real issue with it.

As I walked along the sidewalk toward his shop, he stepped outside and turned my direction. After checking his watch and making me feel even guiltier for bein late, he turned away and walked inside.

Shit.

Shit.

Shit.

I increased my speed to a slow jog and slowed immediately before reaching the window in front of his building. After adjusting my glasses and tugging the bottom of my shorts out of my twat, I pulled the door open and stepped inside. As it had in the past, the shop smelled sterile, causing my nostrils to flare for a moment until they adjusted to the unidentifiable cleaning products.

"You ready?" he asked as soon as I stepped through the door.

"Uhhm yeah. Sorry I'm late. I was actually early, but I was thinking. I think I want a sleeve. I've seen some pictures online and I really like the thought of a sleeve," I said as I began to walk his direction.

"Let's get this done first, have a seat," he said as he turned away.

Don't be mad.

"I'm really sorry I'm late," I said as I walked toward his work station.

I glanced around the empty shop. The work area adjacent to Blake's was a mess. The drawers to the tool box were opened and there were tattoo machines, supplies, and drawings scattered about.

"Where's uhhm," I paused as I continued to look at the mess.

"Tyler?" he asked.

"Yeah, where's Tyler?"

"He got mad and left. He was distracting me. You need to use the bathroom or anything?" he asked as he held the stencil in the air for me to see.

A large coiled snake with the scales on the stomach exposed and the mouth partially opened was neatly drawn on the paper.

"Oh wow. I like that. It amazes me you can just draw something like that," I said.

He widened his eyes and shrugged his shoulders. He seemed short tempered. I hoped my being a few minutes late didn't upset him.

"Oh, I'm sorry. No, I'm ready. I brought water and some protein bars, so I'm good to go," I said.

"Well, have a seat. Actually just lay down on your stomach. We'll do it a little different than last time. You wear a sports bra?" he said as he pointed to the leather chair.

The leather chair was similar to a dentist's chair, and was extended to be flat, resembling a wide leather bed elevated on an aluminum frame. I glanced at the chair and thought of lying on my back in my bra while Blake tattooed something on my hip. For whatever reason, the thought of lying down half naked seemed more intimate than sitting upright. After a short study of the chair, I turned toward Blake and grinned.

"Yes, I did. Are you upset with me? Because I was late?" I asked as

I placed my purse beside the chair.

"No, I'm not mad at you, I'm pissed off at Tyler," he snapped back as he pulled rubber gloves onto his hands.

"Take your shirt off and lay down," he said flatly as he pointed to the chair again.

"You want to talk about it?" I asked.

"About what?"

"Tyler?"

"Tyler's a fucking idiot sometimes. He was saying shit about you, and it made me mad."

I didn't want to act overly interested, but if Blake was sticking up for me when Tyler was talking shit, I wanted to hear about it.

"What did he say?" I asked as I pulled my shirt over my head.

"Just talking shit," he shrugged.

"Like what? I won't get mad, I'm just curious. I don't even know him, it seems funny that he'd say anything," I said as I lowered myself onto the chair.

"He said if you came in here this morning wearing the clothes you wore, you did it to encourage me," he said.

Lying flat on my stomach, I pressed my elbows into the leather and rested my chin in the palms of my hands. I fixed my eyes on him and shook my head lightly, taking complete offense to what Tyler had said, but hoping to keep my cool in my display of my anger.

"Encourage you to what? Jesus. I was on my way home from the gym. If I would have gone home and then came back, it would have been like another hour. He's full of shit. And encourage you? What does that even mean?" I snapped back.

"Don't worry about it. He's gone now it doesn't matter," he said as he leaned against the side of the chair.

Still upset about Tyler saying anything about me, I rolled to my side and gazed up at Blake. His hair was the same usual adorable mess, just spiked a little higher than normal. His eyes were puffy and he looked exhausted, as if he had slept very little the night before. I didn't feel it my place to pry into his personal life, and I guessed it was completely possible that his fight with Tyler had worn on his nerves so much that he was simply worn out.

"So what all did he say?" I asked, "Just tell me, I won't get mad."

He shook his head lightly, grinned, and eventually started to laugh. As he raised his hand to cover his mouth, I realized he had yet to rub his hands together since I had arrived. I began to wonder just what it was that triggered him to rub his hands together in the manner he did so, and as I was preparing to press him a little harder about Tyler, he began to speak.

"He said you were a slut. He said you were wearing those clothes to encourage me to try and fuck you. I explained you weren't like that, and he just kept going on and on about it, swearing you were nothing but a skank," he said.

I sat up in the seat, "A skank? Really? Wow. Wait till I see him."

He shook his head. "Forget it, really. I made him leave for the rest of the day. He'll think about what he said, believe me."

A slut?

Really?

"You know what?" I asked.

He sat on the edge of the chair, reached for my ponytail, and moved it to the side as he studied my back. After a moment of leaning behind me and staring, he sat up straight.

"What's that?" he responded.

"One guy. Just one. That's how many people I've slept with. One. I was with him from my junior year in high school until last year. One. I wonder what Tyler can say about himself? That fucker," I growled.

"Wow, that's impressive," he said as he stood.

He stood at the side of the chair nodding his head. After a moment of what seemed to be deep thought, he continued.

"Holy shit, I'll have to tell him how wrong he was. But Tyler? He's a man whore who's basically addicted to sex. He fucks anything that moves, so he's not one to talk. Just forget about it, you ready?"

"Sure," I said as I relaxed onto my stomach, "That fucker. It just makes me mad. Who's he to say anything?"

"Exactly. Let's just both forget it.

The thought of Tyler calling me a slut or saying I was intentionally trying to lure Blake into something sexual was aggravating. I was conscious of what I was wearing, and I was even a little apprehensive to come in with it on. The reluctance, at least in my mind, confirmed my intention as being more wholesome than whorish.

"Okay," I said.

I closed my eyes as he wiped my back, shaved the area, and pressed the stencil onto my skin. After checking the placement in the mirror, I relaxed onto the chair, and he sat beside me on his stool.

"Ready?" he asked.

I tilted my head to the side and glanced upward. He seemed peaceful and much different than when I arrived. After a few seconds of admiration, I grinned and nodded my head.

"I'm ready. You really enjoy this, don't you?" I asked.

"If you find something you really enjoy, you'll never work another day in your life," he responded. "This isn't work. For me, it's therapeutic. It keeps me at peace."

"I like it. It's weird, but getting a tattoo seems soothing," I responded as I lowered my head.

A song I recognized, *Pearl Jam's Yellow Ledbetter*, began to play. I realized as I absorbed the guitar solo introduction that the music wasn't some special "for tattoo shop only" selections. It was probably music that he had personally chosen.

"I like this song," I said.

"Yellow Ledbetter. I feel that way sometimes," he said.

"How's that?" I asked.

"Ready?" he asked.

I pressed my face into the leather and nodded my head.

"Ready," I mumbled.

The buzzing began, and immediately following the sound, the needle pressed against my skin, causing me to jump slightly.

"You alright?" he asked.

"Fine," I responded.

I tilted my head to the side, "What did you mean you feel like that sometimes?"

"Close to the end," he said over the buzzing, "He says he doesn't know whether he's the boxer or the bag. Sometimes I feel like that."

I thought about what he said, tried to remember the lyrics of the song, and realized for some reason I liked the song despite the fact I had no idea what they were saying.

"I think I feel like that sometimes too," I said.

I closed my eyes and tried to decide based on the feeling of the needle against my skin exactly where he was tattooing. After some time,

I realized I had no idea, and the tattooing, in some respects, caused my skin to feel numb and almost immune to feeling anything with accuracy. It was almost as if I felt the needle in my right arm even though I fully realized it was on my lower left shoulder.

"Have you always been artistic?" I asked.

"Yeah," he chuckled over the sound of the buzzing, "When I was a kid I used to paint the railcars at the tracks downtown. You want to know the coolest thing about that?"

"Sure."

"Seeing one of the cars being pulled along the tracks a few years later with my mural still painted on it," he said.

"That'd be pretty cool. I wonder how many people over the entire United States saw that mural. You know, everywhere it had been," I said.

"Exactly," he responded. "I thought the same thing. I felt like a celebrity, I don't know, like I'd made it into the big leagues. I just remember feeling pretty proud."

"I bet. Yeah, that's pretty cool."

"So you've owned this shop for two years?" I asked.

"Yeah."

"What did you do before this?" I asked.

The buzzing stopped. His stool inched across the floor until he was at my side. As he cradled the tattoo machine in his hand, the expression on his face changed to one of a more serious nature. After a long moment of obvious contemplation, he responded.

"I was a cop," he said flatly.

I raised myself up in the chair slightly. "A police officer? A cop? Like an actual cop?"

He nodded his head.

His face washed with a look of concern. In a matter of seconds, it was almost as if his mind had slipped into memories of the past, thinking of his former profession. I began to feel guilty for asking, and had only been trying to get to know him, but it was obvious thinking about whatever he was thinking about upset him.

"It's an admirable profession," I said softly.

He blinked his eyes, glanced at the tattoo machine, and after a short pause, nodded his head.

"I suppose so," he said.

"What about you?" he asked as he scooted his stool around to the other side of the chair.

"I've uhhm, I've never had a job. During school, my mom wanted me to focus on studies, and after school I was in a relationship with a guy who was pretty well off financially. He didn't really want me out in public, and for sure didn't want me to work. So, I stayed at home unless I was with him," I said.

"Didn't want you out in public? What the fuck was that about? Seriously?" he asked as he began to press the needle onto my back.

"He was pretty protective of me," I responded.

He stopped the tattoo machine and cleared his throat. "That's not protective, Riley. It's controlling, there's a difference."

I found his belief on the issue to be comforting. I had originally felt the same way, but Stephen continued to assure me he was protective, not controlling. Over time, he convinced me it was his protective nature that caused him to prevent me from doing anything alone. Having someone agree with my thoughts on his behavior was reassuring.

"You think so?" I asked.

"Fucking know so. What the fuck was he protecting you from by making you stay at home? I mean, really. Protecting you from life? From exposing yourself to society? Protecting himself from potentially losing you if you bumped into someone who enlightened you into understanding he was a controlling prick, maybe. Ready?"

"Yeah, I'm fine, go ahead. Yeah, he was probably more controlling than most," I agreed.

As he began to work on the tattoo, he continued, speaking just loud enough for me to hear him over the buzzing of the machine and the music.

"I've never really been in a relationship. I've been waiting for the right one to come along I suppose. I always told myself when the right one came along, I'd treat her with respect and truly try to act as if we were equal. I'm sure most guys tell themselves the same shit," he said.

I raised my head slightly, and rested my chin on my clenched fist.

"You've never been in a relationship?" I asked.

"Nope."

"Wow."

"So, what qualities does the right girl have?" I asked.

After a long moment of him continuing to work on the tattoo, he stopped and dipped the needle in the ink. He wiped my shoulder clean, rested his forearm on my side, and paused.

"On the outside? Bold glasses, ponytail, a well-defined waist, but I really don't care about tits. I prefer unpainted fingernails, and she's got to have toes that don't look like little sausages. The toes are important," he said.

My heartbeat immediately increased ten-fold. He had just described me. As I tried to think of how to respond, he continued.

"On the inside, she needs to be kind, forgiving, understanding, and appreciative of art, music, enjoy eating hot dogs as much as sushi, like riding on the back of a motorcycle, and be willing to be tattooed. As far as I'm concerned, there are only two types of people on this earth: those who are tattooed and those who aren't; and I don't trust anyone who doesn't have a tattoo. I'd say that's about it," he said flatly.

"Wow. If I didn't know better, I'd think you just described me," I said jokingly.

"I did," he responded.

My mouth immediately went dry, my body began to tingle, and I felt like I was a little girl again.

As I turned my head to the side and gazed in his direction, he stopped the tattoo machine and grinned.

His eyes were hazel. I hadn't been able to identify the color before, but they were every bit as green as they were brown. As I gazed into his eyes, I felt my heart began to swell with something comparable to pride. I wasn't really prepared for the feeling I felt, and although I had every intention of getting to know more about Blake, I wasn't necessarily ready to have an actual feeling of attraction in the sense I was feeling it. Slightly confused, but pleased with what I was feeling nonetheless, I gazed into his eyes and imagined him kissing me softly.

And for that moment, as he sat and silently returned my gaze, I felt as if we had been pulled a little closer to each other.

Yet.

I wanted more.

BLAKE

Not only had I been making every effort to avoid women I found attractive or tempting, if for some reason I encountered one, it seemed I had been running the other direction. Since I decided they were as much as a problem to me as crack cocaine, I felt it my duty to separate myself from them as quickly as possible. Riley, however, caused me to lower my fists and slowly but curiously walk in her direction.

I had no idea how to pinpoint what it was about her that allowed me to place her in a different category altogether, but it really didn't matter. For whatever reason, my mind decided she was safe for me. Any other woman with her looks, personality, and sense of right and wrong would have long since had my cock between her legs and my hand on the back of her head after the second tattoo. She, on the other hand, seemed to be protected from my sexual advances.

After considerable thought, I decided she had to be special in ways and manners that I wasn't even able to see or even identify. The fact she could share time and space with me, and I wasn't attempting to move forward sexually proved to me she was truly deserving of whatever I was able to offer her beyond sex. In my opinion, she was entitled to learn things about me that no other woman had, and I was eager to share myself with her.

Slowly, but without much real resistance, Tyler was beginning to understand my placement of Riley.

"So, you're trying to tell me you don't even want to fuck her?" he asked.

"You're so fucking stubborn sometimes. I'm not trying to tell you anything. I've told you. Over and fucking over, Dude. No, I don't want to fuck her. I mean I think about it, and yeah, I'd like to fuck her, but not like *fuck* her fuck her. Maybe one day, but not now. You know, if we ended up in a real relationship, yeah. But not now, no. Make sense?" I asked.

"Makes sense, just hard to believe," he responded.

I continued to separate my needles by size, placing them in their respective compartments as I did inventory. After a moment of thinking, I continued speaking to him over my shoulder.

"You know, I think sometimes life, like, puts shit in front of us that we can use to make progress toward a personal perceived perfection as long as we're smart enough to recognize it as being what it is," I said.

"What in the holy fucking hell did that mean? That sounded like some fucking twelve step triple 'p' horseshit right there. *Personal perceived perfection*," he chuckled.

"Fuck you. Just listen. You're getting up and going to work, and doing your deal every day, say, just like me. And you fuck every chick you can. Hell, you even make it a point to try and fuck the ones that don't want to fuck, just to see if you can. Fucking the chick at the gas station who works the register. Fucking the chick at the bar who works the late Tuesday shift. Fucking the meth head that wants a tattoo, but can't save the money. Then, one day, you realize you've got a serious problem. So, you try and abstain. You know, go without sex or whatever. And then some hot as fuck bitch comes in for a tattoo. I mean normally

I'd have been all over her, but for some reason I wasn't," I paused and turned to face him.

"And the reason is that she's different. She's actually like the answer to my problems. She's like an AA meeting for a drunk, only in human form. Being around her makes me not even want to think about other woman. So, she's been put in front of me as a resource or a solution. And it was my recognizing her as being just that that has allowed me to make progress toward actually recovering. It's like I don't even have a problem anymore," I said.

"You're fucking cured?" he coughed.

"No, asshole, not cured. But not actively pursuing other women. It's a huge step in the right direction," I said.

"Suppose so," he agreed.

"So, what did you tell her about yourself? Were you honest?" he asked.

I glanced up from my drawer and nodded my head. "Yeah."

"Completely?" he asked.

"Yeah, completely," I responded.

"Doubt that," he said sarcastically.

"Tell her you were a cop?" he asked.

I nodded my head.

He began to laugh hysterically. After what seemed to be an eternity of breathless laughter, he stumbled to the bathroom. After a few minutes, he came out; no longer laughing, but coughing and trying to catch his breath.

"What?" I asked, "What's so funny?"

"Nothing. Dude, I'm happy for you. Keep doing what you're doing. But one of these days, you'll have to tell her everything, you know that, right?" he asked.

"I will," I said as I pushed the drawer closed.

"No, I mean everything. And be truthful," he said.

I nodded my head again, "See? I'm not even getting upset. It doesn't bother me that you're saying that. Know why? Because I'm comfortable with everything. Don't worry, as soon as I feel like I can trust her one hundred percent, I'll tell her everything."

"Everything?" he asked.

I nodded my head, "Everything."

The sound of the front buzzer caused me to shift my eyes away from Tyler and toward the door. A thirty-something year old MILF with big fake tits came through the door wearing a pair of Daisy Dukes and a wife beater. After swallowing heavily and craning my neck to see her feet, I was shocked and slightly worried that she had extremely thin toes. I quickly turned to face Tyler and winked.

"I'll get this one," I said.

He ran his finger through his thick hair and grinned.

"Seriously? Did you see her toes?" he whispered.

"Yeah," I replied.

"Dude, you're a sucker for thin toes like that, leave her alone. Let me get her," he said under his breath.

I shook my head and took a step in her direction.

"You're serious?" he asked.

"Yeah, to prove a point. Just watch," I said as I turned her direction.

"How can I help you?" I asked as I walked up to the counter that separated the shop from the waiting area.

Now that I was standing directly in front of her, it was pretty obvious she was wearing no bra, nor did she need to. Whoever had performed her augmentation had shoved her tits so full of silicone that the defied the laws of physics and they stood straight up, one nipple directly in the center, and one slightly higher and to her right. As much as I didn't care, my obsessive nature caused me to want to tweak her nipples into their correct locations.

"Hi, I'm Candee, but my friends call me Diamond. I'm a friend of Sandy's. She said I should ask for Blake, are you Blake?" she asked.

Sandy was a single mother who had come in early in the previous winter, wanting a complete back piece done. If I was giving a quote for the tattoo she had requested, it would have been the upside of $2,000, but she negotiated getting it free of charge.

I nodded my head. "Sure am. What can I do for you?"

"Well…" she said.

Roughly thirty blowjobs, a dozen or so good solid fuckings, and an afternoon of fucking Tyler and me simultaneously, she paid for her tattoo, and the three of us were pleased with everything. Since completing the tattoo, I hadn't seen her, but that was typical for the women who chose to trade sex for tattoos. It seemed after it was all over, most of them felt like nothing but a whore, and were embarrassed about what they had chosen to do.

I wondered how many of them regretted it later, as I would expect every time they looked at the tattoo, it would act as a reminder of their willingness to trade their bodies for sex.

"I was thinking about getting a back piece, one almost exactly like Sandy's," she said as she twisted her hips from side to side.

"Oh really?" I asked.

"Yeah, but maybe like a big dragon instead of the peacock she got. But the same size and everything," she said.

71

"I see. It'd be a pretty intricate piece. It could be free-handed, and I could start on it today, or I could draw something up and see what you thought about it, maybe make an appointment for this weekend. Turn around and let me see the width of your back," I said.

She turned around, hooked her thumbs in the pockets of her shorts, and bent slightly at the waist. There was no doubt she was attractive, and in her altered state she was built for one thing and one thing only: fucking. My interest, however, remained solely with Riley. After a quick study of her back, I asked her to turn around.

"You have any scars, birthmarks, or imperfections on your back?" I asked.

She turned her head, peered over her shoulder toward the window. After feeling satisfied no one was passing by, she reached down and pulled off her shirt in one quick yank. Her two cantaloupe sized tits held firm and high on her size two frame. Her nipples looked much worse in the flesh than they did hidden by the thin fabric of her shirt.

"I don't know, you tell me," she said as she slowly turned around.

"You wanting to suck a little cock and maybe give up that little pussy for this tat?" I asked flatly.

She peered over her shoulder. "I'd like to."

"Tyler," I hollered, "This one's for you."

As he hurried toward the front of the shop, I turned away and got my cigarettes. Instead of walking past them again and being forced to see her dumb naked self again, I walked out the back door, sat down on my motorcycle, and lit a cigarette.

Halfway through the cigarette, I took my phone from my front pocket, scrolled to Riley's number, and typed a simple text.

Thinking of you

After reading and rereading it a few times, I decided it was perfect.

I pressed send, grinned at the thought of her reading it, and wondered what would go through her mind when she did. It was actually the first text message I had sent her, and my first step toward anything with her that was beyond total professionalism. As I pushed the phone into my pocket, it beeped.

I bit the butt of the cigarette in my teeth, pulled the phone from my pocket and opened the text message.

I've never stopped

Reading the text caused me to smile from ear to ear. The thought of her thinking of me provided me with an odd sense of satisfaction that everything I was feeling wasn't all for not. As I pursed my lips around the cigarette and inhaled a long drag, I pressed the buttons on the screen.

Coffee?

I pressed send, flicked the cigarette butt into the alley, and exhaled the smoke into the humid evening air. Before the smoke dissipated, the phone beeped again.

Thought you'd never ask

I quickly typed my next message.

Pick you up on the bike?

The response was immediate.

Can't wait 12721 Birchwood. When?

I gazed at the back door and thought of Tyler and the MILF with off centered nipples.

Now?

I pressed send.

Her response caused me to once again grin from ear to ear.

I'll be sitting on the porch waiting

73

I turned on the key, started the motor, and allowed it to warm up to temperature before pulling out of the alley. As I rode past the front of the shop, I slowed to an almost stop and peered inside. Although the blinds were pulled, the east blind wasn't shut completely. The shadows were clear, at least to me, but I knew what I was looking for.

Candee Diamond was bent over Tyler's chair, and he was behind her fucking her like a mad man. I turned to face the street ahead of me and prepared to accelerate. I realized the further away from that nasty bitch I could make myself, the better off I would be. As I gripped the throttle, I couldn't help myself. Similar to passing a terrible accident on the highway, I had to take one last look.

As Tyler continued to pound away he glanced in my direction. Realizing the sound of my exhaust must have gathered his attention, I raised my left hand and waved. He released her hip, raised his right hand, and waved in return. Slightly humored, but even more disgusted, I twisted back on the throttle with my right hand and separated myself from him and Candee as quickly as I was able.

As I rode up the street, my only focus was Tyler's having traded sex for the tattoo. The ride to Riley's house was about ten miles, and took almost twenty minutes in traffic. The entire trip, the MILF being in the shop bothered me. In considering my life's concerns, I realized changing things would only come from making a change within me.

I pulled up in front of her house and she was right where she said she would be, sitting on the porch in her jean shorts, Chuck's, and a worn tee shirt.

As I watched her stand and walk my direction, I decided I would implement a new company policy starting the next day.

Blurred Lines would be a cash only establishment. Trading sex for tattoos would be a thing of the past.

Even for Tyler.

RILEY

My life was a book. The chapters had been my experiences, and although I couldn't alter the portion that had been written, I was prepared to change the tone of the book from the dramatic mess it had been to a love story with a happy ending.

"So what did you think? You enjoy riding?" he asked as he pulled the motorcycle into to the driveway.

"I loved it," I responded. "It was much more fun than I expected."

He flipped a switch beside his right hand and stopped the engine. Feeling a slight bit awkward sitting on the back of the motorcycle and gripping his waist in my hands with the engine off and the motorcycle stationary in the driveway, I released my grip and stared down at my empty hands. I leaned forward until my chin touched the back of his shoulder.

"You want to come in?" I asked.

"I should probably get home. Busy day tomorrow," he responded as he leaned over the left side of the motorcycle.

After he lowered the kickstand, I got off the motorcycle and turned to face him. He relaxed into the seat and rubbed his hands together as frantically as he had in the tattoo shop. As he shifted his eyes from the porch to me and around the yard, his hands never stopped moving. I decided as I watched him that it was a nervous habit, and something about being around me and not having an agenda made him nervous.

"Well…" he began as he turned his head to face me.

"Just for a little bit?" I asked.

His hands stopped moving and he clenched his right hand into a fist. As he raised his hand to his mouth, he exhaled and glanced toward the porch.

While he gazed blankly at the porch, I realized Blake was truthfully only the second man I had spent time with in my adult life; or at least time alone with. Although I had spent my entire life in the presence of a man, that man had been Stephen, and I had no experience beyond him. Being with Blake and doing nothing to speak of was more enjoyable than being with Stephen and doing anything. With Blake, for whatever reason, I felt I was able to relax. Maybe it was that he didn't question me, make demands of me, or require an explanation of my whereabouts while he was at work.

In the time we had spent at the coffee shop I realized I had no idea who I really was or what I enjoyed doing with a man. If someone were to ask me the question, I couldn't accurately respond. Being in Blake's presence was simple and required very little on my part. He seemed satisfied with me, my actions, and my responses to his simple questions. Even though I understood any man who was attentive to my needs would probably be perceived as being worthy of reciprocation on my part, Blake was different.

Or at least I told myself so.

He seemed mysterious to me. In hindsight, it was quite possible anyone would have seemed to be a mystery; but at the time, I was convinced Blake was someone I needed to figure out, and doing so appeared to consume me. The mysterious element combined with his expressed interest in me and his handsome looks were all I needed to convince myself prying further into his life was what I needed to do with all of my available time. And, as I was living off of Stephen's money and didn't have a job, time was something I had plenty of.

"Maybe like ten minutes," he responded as he lowered his hand.

For me to hide my excitement was impossible.

"Ten minutes is great," I said excitedly.

Without warning or excuse, I began walking toward the porch. After stepping onto the first step, I paused and turned toward the driveway. Blake was still sitting on his motorcycle. Once again rubbing his hands together, but much less aggressively this time, he gazed in my direction.

He seemed confused.

Based on what I was able to see, and only on what I was able to see, I would have expected Blake to be an aggressive man who possessed a take-charge attitude. He sat nervously on his motorcycle as proof that judging someone based on their looks alone wasn't an intelligent decision. His appearance made him attractive to me, but his many nervous actions and uncertainty of how to proceed made him even more so.

"Come on, the clock's ticking away," I said playfully.

He stepped off of the bike and glanced around the yard.

"Nice place," he said as he slowly walked up the drive.

"Thanks, I'm just leasing it," I responded.

"Still pretty nice," he said.

"Thank you," I said as I stood on the bottom step and waited for him.

As I reached into my pocket and fished for my keys, he stood on the back side of the porch, as far away from me as he was physically able. After opening the door and stepping inside, I waited as he glanced around at his surroundings and proceeded to slowly walk into the house. After raking his fingers through his hair, he peered into the living room and seemed to survey the furniture.

"Where do you want me to sit?" he asked.

I waved my hand toward the living room. "Wherever, it doesn't matter."

His eyes shifted nervously around the room. "Are we going to sit together?"

"If you want," I said.

"I wasn't sure," he shrugged.

"I mean, if you want to, I'd like to," I said.

"You want something to drink?" I asked.

"I'm good," he responded as he stepped in front of the couch.

I walked past him, sat on the far side of the couch, and patted the cushion beside me. "Sit down, I promise, I won't bite."

"I'm not afraid of you," he said as he sat down a few feet from me.

"I was just joking. So, what are your policies about your clients? You know, like hanging out with your clients?" I asked.

As soon as I spoke, I felt like maybe I should have waited to ask the question. As I sat feeling somewhat foolish for blurting it out without much thought, he responded.

He shook his head. "No policies about that."

"So, we're good?" I asked.

He nodded his head as he crossed his legs. "Yeah, we're good."

I twisted to the side and turned to face him. "You remember I told you'd I'd only been with one guy in my life?"

"Yeah, I remember," he responded as he uncrossed his legs and pressed the palms of his hands onto his thighs.

"Well, just so you know, I'm nervous," I said, even though for some reason I wasn't.

He turned to face me, crossed his legs again, and folded his arms in front of his chest. I glanced at his tattooed knuckles, held my gaze for a moment, and shifted my eyes upward slightly, trying not to focus directly on his face, but well beyond him.

I felt a need to make Blake comfortable, as he was obviously uncomfortable, and was expressing it outwardly. I was sure he was no newcomer to being in the presence of women, and I wondered if my lack of experience with men was exactly what might have been making him uncomfortable, or if it was my age. Although I felt immature at times with Stephen, I felt in the short time I had been away from him I had matured considerably, and was now equal to or beyond other women my age in regard to my level of maturity.

After an extended period of silence, the majority of which I spent gazing at my faux fern and a book case full of books I hadn't read, I shifted my eyes to Blake and decided my repeated explanations of only being with one man were more than likely the driving force of his nervous behavior.

In short, I suspected he didn't know how to proceed with me for fear of causing *me* to feel uncomfortable.

"It shows," he responded.

I leaned into the arm of the couch and widened my eyes slightly.

"Does it?" I asked.

He nodded his head. "Your body language."

Although I took exception to his statement, I said nothing. After a short pause, I opted to change the subject slightly.

"You know, I like being around you. Even though I may act nervous, you make me feel comfortable. It's nice being around someone who doesn't demand things of me or push me around. I just might get used to this if you're not careful," I said.

He uncrossed his legs and turned to face me. "Oh really? Get used to it, huh?"

I nodded my head and grinned. He glanced down at the cushion between us.

He intertwined his fingers and cracked his knuckles. After inhaling a slow breath through his nose, he exhaled and glanced upward.

"Wait. Push you around, what do you mean?" he asked.

"My ex, he used to get kind of rough with me sometimes," I said.

"What do you mean?" he asked.

I shrugged my shoulders. "I don't know, he was just a mean person."

"Well, what do you mean? Define rough," he said.

I shrugged again and considered what to tell him. After a short moment, I decided there was no harm in telling him the truth.

"Well, I already told you we got together when I was young," I paused, exhaled, and adjusted my position on the couch.

"He uhhm. After a year or so, he'd get mad at me and shove me or slap me, and he…"

He uncrossed his arms and his eyes went wide.

"He'd slap you?" he asked.

I nodded my head.

He stood from his seat and faced the far wall. After a moment, he turned around and glared down at me.

"Seriously?" he asked.

I thought I had already shared my stories of Stephen's violent behavior with Blake when I was at the tattoo parlor. Based on his reaction, it was apparent I had not. I fixed my eyes on his, pursed my lips, and nodded my head.

"I don't like that. Not at all," he said.

"I didn't like it either. That's why I left," I responded.

He lowered himself onto the couch, this time right beside me with his leg almost touching mine. I glanced at his leg, making note of his close proximity, and he immediately began to reposition himself. I placed my hand on his thigh, leaned to the side, and as awkward as it seemed doing so, kissed him lightly on the lips. Although it was apparent by his expression the kiss caught him off guard, I continued. I kissed him again, this time fully on the lips and with a little more aggression.

He kissed me in return, and after a few seconds, the awkwardness of it all diminished. Almost immediately, we were making out on the couch like a couple of prepubescent unknowing teens. The excitement of it all was beyond what I would have imagined, and far more than I expected kissing anyone would ever be. Be it the fact I initiated it, or because it was with someone I really enjoyed spending time with, I didn't know nor did I care. At that moment, kissing Blake was more satisfying than anything I could ever remember experiencing. As we continued, his hands eventually found their resting place, one on my waist, and one on my right bicep.

When I was young, I was an avid movie watcher, and always chose a romance over any other movie. *Love Actually, The Notebook, The Proposal, When Harry Met Sally, Pretty Woman, Dear John*, and *Say Anything* were among my favorites. After countless movies and much anticipation, I expected my first kiss to resemble what the movies depicted. I was surprised to find that, at least for me, kissing wasn't as enjoyable in person as it was expressed in the movies.

Until now.

Kissing Blake was something completely different. With my head spinning and my mind grasping at the new sensation and attempting to identify it, I continued to kiss him, not wanting the newfound pleasure to stop. As my stomach began to swirl in circles from the escalating sexual tension, I reluctantly paused for a much needed breath.

As our lips parted, I glanced down and into his lap. His excitement was apparent, as his cock had his jeans stretched to a point of ripping through the denim if we continued. It was pretty obvious he was well-endowed, and after my having caught a glimpse of his level of arousal, I decided to let him know my thoughts.

I was so far beyond being sexually aroused that I really would have had a difficult time explaining to anyone other than myself how I felt. Sometimes, I decided, actions are better than the spoken word. I leaned forward, pressed my lips to his, and reached for the denim tent he was pitching. As soon as my hand encompassed his swollen rod, I squeezed lightly, and he instantly jumped from the couch.

"I really need to get," he said as he jumped up.

"Did I do something wrong?" I asked as I wiped my mouth with the back of my hand.

. "No, I need to go check the shop. You know, lock the door," he said as he pressed the heel of his palm against his crotch.

I gazed down at his feet. "I'm sorry if I…"

"No," he said as he shook his head from side-to-side. "I just need to get."

"Okay," I said as I stood from the couch.

Regardless of his reason, I felt like an idiot.

"Are you sure…"

He raised his hand in the air and shook his head.

"I enjoyed it," he said.

He leaned forward, kissed me lightly, and turned toward the door.

I stood in slight shock as I heard his motorcycle start, and collapsed onto the couch as he rode away. Contrary to what he had said, I felt that my physical advancement was the sole reason for him leaving.

Frustrated with myself, but in no way regretting the kiss, I sat on the couch and wondered what my next step should be. As I crossed my legs and stared at the plastic fern, the answer came to me.

I needed to do what I had become almost a master at doing since I left Stephen.

I needed sexual relief.

And I needed it promptly.

BLAKE

I sat on the couch and stared at the bookcase. Some days were easier to talk than others, and if I measured the days on a scale of one through ten, ten being the most difficult for me to talk, this one would have come in at roughly nine and a half.

"So, do you feel like you've lied to her?" he asked.

I sat and stared blankly at the books. It was quite possible it was a ten. He sat silently and waited. After an extended period of silence, he cleared his throat.

"Have you read all of these?" I asked.

"We've discussed the books multiple times, Blake. I have read every one of them, yes. Now, back to my question, 'do you, or did you feel that you may have lied to her? And, if so, how does that make you feel?'" he asked.

I stared at the books, and although I had counted them many times in the past, I began to count them again. After another extended period of silence, I reached a total, and counted them again to make certain.

Two hundred and seventeen. That's not really that many.

"How long did it take you?" I asked, still focusing on the books.

He cleared his throat again. "Most were read over the course of my education. A few before and a few since. Several years."

After a few minutes, I turned to face him, glanced at the clock, and made note of the fact that almost twenty minutes had passed.

"If your concern is time, Mr. West, I'll assure you I have much more time today than normal. We'll sit here until my questions are answered. Now, I'll ask again…"

"Kind of," I interrupted.

"Kind of what?" he asked.

"Kind of feel like that," I responded.

"Kind of feel like what? Describe your feelings," he said.

"Shit," I said.

"Your feelings are shit?" he asked.

"I feel like shit. That's what you asked. How do I feel, that's what you asked. I feel like shit. Write that down," I said.

"Well, to take a few steps back, I asked, more specifically, if you felt like you had lied to…" he paused and glanced down at his note pad.

"Riley," he said.

I sat up in my seat and leaned forward slightly, resting my elbows on my knees as I glared at him.

"Take her name off your little fucking pad," I said.

"I merely made note of…"

"Take it off," I said flatly.

"My notes stay here. With me. There's no harm in…"

"Take her name off your fucking pad," I demanded.

He gazed down at the pad and began to scribble. I stood from my seat. As he noticed me stand, he placed the pad on his desk and pushed his seat away from the desk.

"Sit down, Mr. West," he said.

"Take her name off the fucking pad. You have no right to write her name down. We were just talking. You weren't even fucking writing when we were talking, you wrote the fucker down later. You fucking cheated," I snapped.

"If I erase it, scratch it out, or toss the sheet in the trash, I still retain the memory of what you said. The longer you make an issue of it, and of her name, the more permanent it will be etched in my mind. Now, let's get back to what we were speaking of. But first, sit down," he said.

I studied him for a moment, exhaled a shallow breath, and sat down. He had a valid point. No matter what I did or said, he already knew Riley's name. My best chance at any kind of recovery from his attack would be to change the subject.

I crossed my legs and focused on the bookcase. After a pause long enough to irritate him I shifted my eyes toward his desk. "Work's been steadily picking up."

He glared at me and picked up his pad. As he began to scribble, my blood pressure began to rise.

"Okay, yeah. I don't know. I felt like maybe I should have said something, but it isn't necessarily the type of shit you run and tell someone you're trying to get to know. But I sure as fuck didn't lie to her. I just didn't tell her. And if you're going to do any more scribbling on your little pad, you can write 'Blake didn't tell her yet', not 'Blake isn't going to tell her'. Got it?"

"Understood. So, you do expect to see her again?" he asked.

I nodded my head.

He began to scribble.

"Hold the fuck up. You need to set that fucking pad to the side. I'm about sick and tired of you scribbling on that fucker. Can we just talk?" I asked.

"Would it be safe to say you are feeling slightly guilty for not having told Riley the truth yet? I do understand you have every intention of telling her everything, but you feel guilty about not having divulged everything yet, is that correct?" he asked.

"If you say so," I responded.

"I want you to tell me. Tell me how it makes you feel that you've decided to wait to tell her everything."

"It makes me feel like I'm a pretty smart fucker, that's how it makes me feel," I said as I reached for my glass of water.

"Oh, and how so?" he asked as he reached for the pad.

I shook my head at the thought of him doing any more scribbling.

"Because if I would have just blurted out my life history, she might have run away. But because I didn't tell her, and we talked a few times without her knowing anything, I think she likes me. So, if I tell her now, she might just shrug her fucking shoulders and say so fucking what. That's why," I said.

He picked up his pen, tapped the end of it against lip for a moment, and then began to carefully write on the pad.

"Blake's a smart fucker, and he's making big time progress. That's what you wrote, right?" I asked.

"Where's the fucking music? There's no music. What's the fucking deal today? It's like fuck with Blake day, huh? Turn the music on," I said as I glanced around the room.

"The music is a program that is time based. It has shut down for the day," he responded.

I glanced around the room and eventually fixed my eyes on him.

"Turn it back on," I said flatly.

He shrugged his shoulders. "It's out of my control."

I sighed a phony sigh of irritation. As I inhaled another deep breath

90

and intended to force another sigh, he cleared his throat. It was his way of attempting to gather my attention; he did it all the time.

"Now, let's discuss your meetings," he said.

"What'd you write on your little pad?" I asked.

He cocked one eyebrow. "The meetings, Mr. West. Let's discuss the meetings."

"You know. Sometimes you call me Blake, and sometimes you call me Mr. West. How do you decide which one to use?" I asked.

He glared.

"Are you still wearing the cross?" he asked.

I reached toward my chest, tapped the piece of silver with the tip of my finger and shook my head.

He scribbled on his pad.

"Are you ready to discuss the meetings, Mr. West?" he asked.

I nodded my head once. "Okay by me, Patrick."

"You're still attending the AA meetings?" he asked.

"As a matter of fact, Mr. Racine, I do. Once a week, maybe twice, it depends on my moods," I responded.

He widened his eyes slightly as he rolled the pen between his thumb and forefinger, studying me the entire time. Eventually he tilted his head to the side. "And you're of the opinion, or at least you were, that they are helping you cope with your addictions?"

"That's my take on it, yeah," I said.

"Interesting. Do you still feel that way?" he asked.

"Well, Patrick, it sure seems to be the case. The meetings help me cope," I responded.

"Do you find today's session annoying, Blake?" he asked.

"Not anymore, Mr. Racine," I said as I stood from my seat.

"Mr. West, sit down," he said in a stern tone.

As I walked toward the door I reached into my pocket, pulled out the key to my Harley, and clutched it in my hand. As I pulled the door open, I paused and turned to face him.

"Next time I'm here, make sure the music's playing. I'm not fucking around. I don't want to talk to you if there's no music. Listening to you in the silence is fucking irritating. Write that down, Patrick," I said.

As he centered the pad on his desk and began to write, I grinned. I really didn't care so much if the music was on or off, I had just become accustomed to listening to it. Having him fully understand my thought processes wasn't ever something I was interested in doing.

Keeping him guessing was much more fun.

"Mr. West, I would appreciate it if…"

I cleared my throat and interrupted him from speaking. "That's another thing, don't call me that anymore."

He fixed his eyes on mine and waited.

"I'm fucking tired of the back and forth shit. Call me Blake. Or you can call me Boss. Or Brainiac. Yeah, that works. Brainiac. I like that," I said with a nod.

And I turned and walked out the door.

RILEY

Growing up, there were times when I was aggravated with my mother, but regardless, I always loved her. She despised Stephen, and we often disagreed about my relationship with him, his treatment of me, and her belief that he was with me for sexual reasons alone. In the end, she was correct in all respects, a quality I think all mothers must possess. Admitting she was right was easy for me, because admitting it allowed me to accept that Stephen truly was the controlling prick she had always believed him to be.

"So, how old is he?" she asked.

"I don't know, but before you say anything, believe me, it doesn't matter," I said.

"Why doesn't it?" she asked.

I shrugged my shoulders. "Because age really doesn't matter, and it shouldn't. But I guess because he's not as old as Stephen, and because you're really going to like him."

"We'll see about that. You said he owns a tattoo shop downtown?" she asked over her cup of coffee.

"Yep, and he doesn't drink, doesn't use drugs, and he's not like Stephen at all," I assured her.

My relationship with my mother had always been one where I could - and did - tell her everything. I found the open line of communication we shared to be therapeutic, never really held anything in reserve, and was always willing to listen to what she had to say; deciding afterward if her opinion was something worthy of considering or implementing in my life. In complete contrast to any other girl my age, I could truly claim my mother was my best friend.

"Well, I like that about him already, as long as it's true," she said.

I clasped my hands around my coffee cup and considered my response.

"Well, he came over the other day and we were making out on the couch. You know, just kissing, but for a really long time. So, I glanced down, and he was rock hard. So, I…"

She raised her hand in the air as if she'd heard enough. As she began to chuckle I continued.

"You asked, Mother. So, anyway, I decided to grab it. And I did. He immediately jumped up, denied me the cock, and went back to work," I said.

"Well that's a first. And good for him," she said with a nod.

"What does that mean?" I asked.

"Stephen forced himself on you from the beginning and never let up. If this guy at least has the courage and the ability to walk away from you groping him, he's much better than Stephen, at least in that regard," she responded as she raised her cup of coffee in the air.

"I didn't grope him. I grabbed his junk," I said with a laugh.

She shook her cup of coffee in front of me, as if offering a toast. I lifted my cup.

"Here's to tattoo artists with courage," she said.

"Courage and a big bulge," I said as I clanked my cup against hers.

"Riley Jaye Campbell," she snapped back.

"I'm telling you," I said.

She took a sip of coffee, shook her head from side to side, and lowered the cup to the table.

"Now, that, I don't need to know," she said.

I narrowed my eyes slightly, grinned and nodded my head once. "I'll keep it a secret."

"As it needs to be," she said.

"So, still not a word from Stephen?" she asked.

I shook my head, "Not a single one."

"Good," she said as she stood from her seat.

"You sure you don't want anything to eat?" she asked.

"No," I responded. "I ate some yogurt before I came."

"You're not eating enough. You look thin," she said over her shoulder as she walked to the refrigerator.

"I look thin because I'm healthy. I've been at the gym every morning since I left Stephen," I said.

She opened the door to the refrigerator, peered inside, and as she rummaged around for a snack, spoke.

"Well, going to the gym doesn't make you healthy. But going to the gym and eating properly might," she said.

"I'm eating properly, Mother," I said.

"If you say so," she said as she pulled her head from the refrigerator.

"What did you come up with?" I asked as she carried a plastic container toward the counter.

"Cantaloupe," she responded.

"Fork me," I said.

She shook her head from side-to-side as she grabbed two forks and a bowl. After dumping the contents of the container into the bowl, she walked back to the table and set it between us. As she handed me the fork, I shrugged my shoulders and glared.

She widened her eyes. "What?"

I stood from my seat, walked to the stove, and grabbed the salt. As I sat down at the table, salt shaker in hand, she shook her head again.

"Not on my half," she said as she covered half of the bowl with her hand.

I shook the shaker over the bowl, making sure to cover her hand with as much salt as possible. After a few extra shakes, I placed it to the side, and stabbed a piece of cantaloupe with my fork.

"That's a good cantaloupe," I said as I chewed the melon.

"Got it at the farmer's market," she responded. "Good, huh?"

I nodded my head and stabbed another piece. "Yep."

As we sat and devoured the entire bowl of cantaloupe together, I realized how much I had missed my mother during my time with Stephen. Although I continued to see her throughout my relationship with him, I didn't see her as frequently, nor was I as open with her as I typically was. Our time together was short, and our talks were brief and almost meaningless.

Although she was my mother, we could easily pass for sisters, and often did. She looked much younger than her thirty-nine years of age, and depending on my makeup and what I was wearing, I could look a little older than my age. She was a very attractive woman, blonde, and no differently than me, had a lanky body and nice boobs.

I had always suspected the only reason she was single was because she wanted to be, not because she had to be. When I started high school and she was thirty-one, all of my male friends claimed she was "hot", and often made excuses to come over and stare at her.

"Why don't you have a boyfriend?" I asked..

"I don't need one," she responded.

"Everyone needs someone," I said.

"Well, I don't," she responded as she stood.

After grabbing the bowl and our two forks, she carried them to the sink. She stood for some time, gazing out the window before coming back to the table and sitting down.

"I suppose it's the same as it's always been, each time you've asked. I still love your father. Being with someone else would never amount to anything but friendship. It wouldn't be fair. I loved, and still love your father," she said.

My father died as a result of a tragic accident when I was in kindergarten. My mother lived, walking away with nothing more than a scar on her neck from the shards of glass. Although the curious side of me always wanted to know more, I was unable to find out any details, as the internet had yet to be developed for widespread use in 1998 when the accident happened.

My mother's explanation of a truck running a red light, a loud metallic crunch, and the sound of breaking glass was all I knew of my father's death.

"All I've ever wanted was for you to be happy," I said as I stood.

She glanced upward, narrowed her gaze, and pointed at my chair. "I am happy. Where are you going?"

"I just wanted to give you a hug," I said.

"Okay," she said as she stood, "But you can't leave. I want to hear more about this Blake character."

"About his bulge?" I whispered as I held her in my arms.

"No, about everything else," she said as she released me.

"You said he rode a motorcycle. Have you been on it yet?" she asked as she sat down.

I nodded my head and grinned, "It's awesome."

"Did you wear a helmet?" she asked.

I glanced down at the legs of the table, knowing she would not like my response, but fully realizing I couldn't lie to her.

"No," I responded.

"Riley Jaye," she gasped.

"Mom, he didn't have one…"

She glared at me. "Not again. I'm not losing you to a motorcycle accident because you weren't sensible enough to wear a helmet."

"Okay," I said.

"Promise me," she said.

"I promise," I whined.

"Okay. Now, tell me everything you know about him."

"Everything?" I grinned.

"Everything but the bulge," she said with a laugh.

"Well, he's tall, but not like *tall*. Maybe six foot-ish. And he's got a little beard thing going on some of the time. You know, a few days growth. He's covered in tattoos; all up and down his arms, hands, knuckles, and even one kind of on his neck, but not like all up on it. But he doesn't look like a thug, he's really cute, mom. He, uhhm, he always looks serious, like he's thinking. He squints his eyes a lot, and when he's doing it, I can tell he's thinking," I paused for a moment and lifted my cup of coffee to my mouth.

I took a drink of the lukewarm coffee, winced at the temperature, and continued.

"He owns his own tattoo shop, and he has a guy who works for him,

98

Tyler, and the guy's a complete dick. He doesn't drink and he doesn't use drugs, but he smokes," I said.

"Pot?" she asked.

"No. Cigarettes," I responded.

"He rides a motorcycle, and I think he said he doesn't even have a car. It seems like he told me that," I said.

"Well, that's kind of strange," she said.

"Oh, and his eyes. They're like brown and green at the same time. Like equal amounts of each, it's crazy," I said.

"Hazel," she said.

"I know, Mother. But not like just hazel, they're crazel," I said.

She scrunched her nose and stared. "Crazel?"

"Yeah, crazy hazel," I said with a laugh.

"It's nice seeing you happy again. And I see you're wearing your glasses. That's a change," she said.

"Well, Stephen hated them. Blake freaking loves 'em. So, I'm wearing them again," I said.

I didn't bother going into detail about my eye being scratched severely, and the eye doctor saying I may never be able to wear contacts for any length of time again. My mother despised Stephen's treatment of me, and another reminder of his violent nature would not do either of us any good. I was over him, he was leaving me alone, and forgetting him was best for both of us.

"I like them, too," she said.

"He's just really reserved and kind of like nervous all the time, it's cute," I said.

"Parents? Does he have a good relationship with his parents?" she asked.

I gazed down at the table for a moment, glanced upward, and shrugged my shoulders.

"I don't know. He hasn't mentioned them."

"Well, I hope if you two end up seeing each other that he's nice to you," she said.

"I think we *are* seeing each other," I said with a nod of my head.

"You think so?" she asked as she stood from her seat.

And, although Blake and I hadn't discussed it, in my mind we were.

"Yes," I said.

And I hoped he believed the same.

BLAKE

As pleasing everyone would never happen, pleasing myself became priority. I determined if I pleased myself, pleasing those around me was easy. Their pleasure came from being exposed to me and seeing me genuinely happy. I found a good mood and a smile to be contagious, more so than even malaria, but much more enjoyable.

There were times truly pleasing myself required sacrificing others. Realizing when those sacrifices needed to be made and recognizing the people who were best suited to be tossed from my life was crucial to my success.

And, at this juncture in my life, my success was the only thing I was concerned with.

I screwed the last screw in the frame and took a few steps back. The sign was perfect, and added to the stand-offish nature I always wanted to possess in the shop. As I placed the cordless drill in the box and clasped it closed, I heard the back door open and slam shut.

"What's with slamming the door?" I asked as I peered over the partition.

"Musta been the wind," Tyler mumbled.

"Okay," I said.

"What're you doing up there?" he asked.

"Posting a new sign," I said as I took one last glance at the sign.

"Raising prices?" he asked as he unlocked his box.

"Nope, prices are fine. Just clarifying the rules," I responded.

"What rules?" he asked.

"Shop rules," I said.

"Huh," he murmured as he turned my direction.

He sauntered to the front of the shop, stepped behind me, and read the sign out loud in a light whisper.

BLURRED LINES

NO use of cellphones beyond this partition

NO children

NO one under 18 beyond this partition

NO I won't use your sketch or stencil

NO checks, trading, or bartering

NO food in the shop

NO tattoo without a valid ID

NO drunks

NObody here cares how cheap your last tattoo was

NO crying, whining, or bitching

YES tipping makes it hurt less

"No checks, trading, or bartering, huh?" he asked.

"That's right," I said.

"Starting when?" he asked.

"Starting," I paused and glanced at my watch. "About ten minutes ago."

"Are you fucking kidding me? Jesus, Blake. Well, good thing Candee Diamond is under the old set of rules," he said as he walked around me.

I began to walk toward my work station. "Old rules no longer apply,"

I said over my shoulder.

"Good thing we already worked out the bartering, and she won't be using a check. If she fucks me again, it'll only be because she liked the cock," he said.

"No sex in the shop," I said.

"Didn't see that on the sign, bro," he said as he sat down.

"Don't need to write it on the sign," I said.

He swiveled his stool around to face me. "No sex?"

"That's right," I said.

"Applies to you too, right?" he asked.

I nodded my head.

He laughed, turned his stool halfway around, and whistled a long shrill whistle.

"We'll see how long that lasts with Riley coming in and out of this motherfucker like a junkie at a methadone clinic," he said.

"Excuse me?" I said.

"You heard me," he said.

I shook my head, decided to keep my mouth shut, and dropped the drill into the bottom drawer of my box. As I pushed the drawer closed, he turned his stool around again.

"You go see her the other day? When you got mad and left?" he asked.

"I wasn't mad, but yeah, I did," I said.

"You fuck her?" he asked.

He was beginning to irritate me. Knowing my best countermeasure was to keep from losing my temper, I picked up the cling wrap and began wrapping my chair.

"Sure didn't," I responded.

"She suck your dick?" he asked.

"Nope," I said.

"She give you a hand job?" he asked.

"No, and who the fuck gets a hand job once they're over the age of fourteen anyway?"

"All types of people. Ever heard of a happy ending?" he asked.

I didn't respond.

"You kiss her?" he asked.

I nodded my head as I continued to wrap the chair in the sheets of transparent plastic.

"So you kissed her and she didn't do anything?" he asked.

"I didn't say that. But what she did or didn't do is none of your business," I responded.

"Since fucking when do you keep things from me, Dude? I fucking swear. So what happened? You kissed and that's it? What are you, twelve?" he asked.

"Fuck you," I responded.

"No, fuck you. She yanked your rod, didn't she?"

I shook my head, tore off the last section of plastic wrap, and pressed it into the leather.

"Nope," I said as I tossed the carton of wrap in the drawer of my box.

"She sucked that motherfucker, I know she did. She's got those DSLs. I bet that bitch can suck a marble through a straw," he said.

I stood, turned to face him, and raised my index finger in the air. "That's enough."

"She sucked that dick. I knew it," he said.

I continued to glare.

"Did she swallow?" he asked.

I bit my bottom lip and attempted to keep my temper at bay. After a moment, he continued.

"Fuck, yes. Gotta love a bitch that swallows," he said.

"She didn't swallow," I said through my teeth.

"Oh?   A spitter, huh? Where'd she spit it? Did she run to the bathroom, or take her time and sit with it in her mouth for a while before she dipped out on ya?"

"She just touched it," I said.

"She played with the cum? Fuck, Dude, that's hot. Like with the tip of her finger, or her tongue?"

"She touched my junk. Through my jeans," I said.

"Wait? What? She touched it? Like a through the jeans rub and tug?" he asked.

I nodded my head.

"Oh hell no. Not since eighth grade. That's unacceptable. Wait till I see this bitch. I'm going to give her a proper instruction manual on what to do and not to do with a grown man's cock. I knew that little bitch was a youngster, but holy fuckballs. That's unacceptable," he said.

"You're not going to say a word to her," I said.

"Don't bet on it," he said over his shoulder as he frantically pulled open the drawers to his box.

"Here we go, pen and paper ready. I'm going to draw stick figures to keep it from being too graphic. What should I name it? You know, the title?" he asked.

"Name what?" I asked as I began to walk in his direction.

"Her instruction manual." he responded.

"If you say one word to her about this…"

He shrugged his shoulders. "Free country."

I stepped behind him, craned my neck over his shoulder, and glanced down at his note pad. A standing stick figure with an erect stick dick stood over a stick woman on her knees with her head impaled on his cock. The cock was all the way to her stick throat, depicted on the paper as a dashed line once it entered her "O" shaped mouth.

"Give me that," I said as I reached for the pad.

He yanked the pad to the side, jumped from his stool, and ran to the front of the shop.

"No way, Dude. She needs to learn the proper way to handle a man's junk. A through the pants rub and tug is reserved for middle school. You'll thank me later," he said.

The thought of Tyler doing anything to jeopardize my relationship with Riley was unacceptable. Riley was good for me, and I suspected I could also be good for her. Together, we would be nothing but goodness. I looked so forward to the next time I was able to see her, and I would be damned if Tyler's insensitive sense of humor was going to come into play in our next meeting.

Enough was enough.

"Give it to me," I demanded.

He shook his head.

"You're fired," I said.

"Fired? You can't fire me, you need me," he screeched.

"You're…"

"Fired…"

"Dude…" he whined.

"Seriously, I'm tired of the bullshit. Get your shit and get out now," I said as I pointed toward the door.

"Here, take it," he said as he extended his arm.

The pad dangled loosely from his fingers.

"Get out," I bellowed.

With wide eyes and a shaking lower lip, he stood and stared. I turned toward his work station, opened the drawers to his box, and shoved everything that belonged to him in the box. I grabbed the handle on the end of the box and drug it across the concrete floor and to the front door.

"Last chance to part as friends," I said as I pointed to his box.

"Dude, don't..."

I pushed the door open, shoved his box onto the side walk, and released the door. As the door swung closed, he stood with his mouth agape and stared at his box.

"You're serious," he said under his breath.

"Dead serious," I responded.

He lowered his shoulders and began to walk toward the rear of the shop.

"I'll give you about sixty seconds to turn around and get out of here, or I'm calling the cops," I said.

"The fucking cops? It's like that?" he asked.

"It is now," I responded.

"I can't believe you let a chick get between us," he said.

"Out," I said as I pointed toward the door.

And, without incident, he turned and walked out the door.

Although I realized there would be times when I missed Tyler, for me to make progress with Riley and have our relationship be healthy, safe, and without the constant pressures associated with sex, Tyler needed to go.

I turned away and walked toward my work station, feeling emptier than I expected. I glanced over my shoulder, and although his box remained on the sidewalk in front of the shop, he was nowhere to be seen.

As I gazed down at the cellophane wrapped chair, I realized I didn't have an appointment booked for the morning, and had wrapped the chair out of nothing more than habit. While I considered unwrapping it, The Weeks began to play over the sound system. One of my favorite tracks, *Hold It Kid*, was a difficult one for me to listen to, but enjoyable nonetheless. As I became immersed in the song and slowly began to slip into a somber mood, the buzzer from the front door startled me.

A guy wearing a leather MC vest came through the door, glanced around, and gazed down at the sign I had added earlier.

"Nice sign," he said.

"Appreciate it," I said as I walked toward the partition. "What can I help you with?"

"Tool box out on the side walk in front of the door, you leave that there? Someone'll steal it for sure as soon as the sun goes down," he said as he tossed his head toward the door.

"No, fired a guy a bit ago. It's his. He'll be back to get it at some point, I'm sure," I said.

"Alright. Well, I need a piece touched up, and want a couple small pieces. One of the fellas came in here the other day, maybe a week or so ago, and had you do some work on his prison tats. You covered a few of them up for him. He recommended you, said you didn't have a shop minimum. Most of the other shops along here won't do a small piece," he said.

"Big guy, covered in prison tats, did a five year state bit on a gun charge. He went by..." I paused and thought of his name, which was quite unique.

"He went by Corn Dog. Good dude," I said with a nod.

"What do you need touched up?" I asked.

He pulled up his shirt sleeve and pointed to a tattoo on his bicep. Cursive script spelled the phrase *The Devil Looks After His Own*, but a few of the letters had worn over the years and were showing their age.

"I can touch that up and make it look new. No changes?" I asked.

"No changes," he said flatly.

"What's the new work?" I asked.

"Want a couple of knuckle tats," he said.

"I'll be honest with you. Knuckle tats are a bitch. I'll do my best, but I can't guarantee it won't blow out. Anyone who gives you a guarantee is a fucking liar. I'll guarantee anything else, and I'll do my best with them, but there's a risk," I said.

"Alright. I want a skull on this finger," he said as he extended the middle finger of his right hand.

He lowered his hand and turned the middle finger of his left hand up. "And an "A" on this one in Old English script."

"Sounds easy enough. How's seventy five for everything sound?" I asked.

"Sounds like you're a reasonable man," he said.

"When do you want to do it?" I asked.

He shrugged his shoulders. "When do you have time?"

"Now? It'll take forty-five minutes on the arm, and fifteen on the knuckles."

"Sounds good. Name's Slice," he said as he extended his right hand.

"Blake," I said.

I reached over the counter and shook his hand. He was a rough looking man with a strong jawline, a few days growth of beard, and a powerful chest. He looked like the man the director would choose to portray a biker in a Hollywood movie about a biker because he looked the part and did so very well. I pulled a waiver from the drawer, grabbed a pen, and placed them on the countertop in front of me.

"Formality," I said as I pushed the piece of paper across the counter.

"Understood," he said as he reached for the pen.

After a moment he slid the sheet and pen over the counter and crossed his arms.

"You alright with taking your shirt off? We could roll it up, but I'd hate to have it come down on piece we're reworking. Maybe just go without it, but you could wear the vest for the rest of the day," I said.

He shrugged his shoulders. "Long as a few scars don't bother you."

"Never have, don't know why they would now," I responded.

"Where do you want me?" he asked.

"Follow me," I said.

As he walked beside me, he removed his vest, pulled off his tee shirt, and tossed it on the end of the chair. As he began to slip his arms through the arm holes in the vest, I turned to face him. His entire back was covered in scars, some of which were a foot long. He looked like he'd been cut intentionally by someone who wasn't too fond of him.

As with all bikers I had met, he'd come by his club name honestly. As I turned the other direction, he snapped the buttons on his vest and turned around.

"Just have a seat and we'll get started," I said as I sat on my stool.

He folded his tee shirt neatly, set it aside, and sat down facing me. As I slid my stool to the side and reached for the ink cabinet, I spoke over my shoulder.

"Black on everything?" I asked.

"Yep," he responded.

I grabbed a tube of ink, squirted out enough for the three tattoos, and pulled a fresh needle from the drawer and remove the wrapper. As I inserted the needle in the machine and adjusted it, the door buzzer went off again.

I'd gone from deserted to Grand Central Station in fifteen minutes.

I glanced toward the door and was pleasantly surprised to see Riley.

"You alright with a little company for a few minutes?" I asked.

"I'm a lot of things, but modest isn't one of 'em. Okay by me," he said.

"Come on back," I said as I waved my arm.

Riley walked up behind him, stopped a few feet short, and grinned as her gaze met mine. Dressed in worn jeans, her Chuck's, and a snug fitting short-sleeved button down shirt, she looked fantastic.

"Uhhm, there's a tool box on the sidewalk," she said as she walked toward the rear of the shop.

"I fired Tyler," I responded.

"Oh, holy shit," she gasped.

I shrugged my shoulders. "It was inevitable, no big deal. Your hair looks great."

"Just got it done. All one color," she said.

"Well, it looks fucking awesome."

Slice turned his head slightly, paused, and twisted his upper body to face Riley.

"Riley Campbell?" he asked.

She shifted her eyes toward him.

"Oh shit. Uhhm. Wow. Uhhm. Axton, right?" she asked.

"Good memory. How the hell are you? I haven't seen you in years," he said as he stood and opened his arms wide.

"Good. Actually, that's a lie. I'm great," she said as she hugged him.

"Your mother?" he asked.

"She's good, as always. Actually, I just left there," she said.

"I saw her a few weeks back, but just waved as we rode past. Hell, I bet I haven't seen you since you were in high school. You still pissing off your mom and seeing that attorney?" he asked.

"No, he's long gone," she said.

"Probably best for you and your mother both," he said.

"Yeah, probably so. I met this guy when I was about fourteen," Riley said.

She walked around the end of the chair, turned to face him, and shook her head. "One of the members of his club lives down the street from my mother, and one day we were standing in the driveway trying to figure out how to change a flat. So, they were riding by, what, about ten of you?"

"Or more," he responded.

"Well, so we were in the driveway with the jack and all the stuff, and neither of us knew what we were doing, and they turned around, pulled in front of the house, and stopped. Mom and I were scared to death. So they're all neatly parked in front of the house, and this guy got off his motorcycle, walked up the driveway, and just started changing the flat tire. He didn't even say anything until he was done. And ever since, he'd just stop by to make sure we were doing okay. The entire time I was in high school he stopped by once a month or so and just asked if we needed anything. Don't let his size or looks fool you, Blake. He's one of the nicest guys you'll ever meet. I can't believe I just bumped into you."

I grinned and glanced at them both. "That's a good story."

"Guess what else?" Riley chuckled as she studied him.

"What's that?" I asked.

"They come by at Christmas and hang mom's Christmas lights. Then they come take them down." She paused and turned to face Axton. "You guys still do that?"

"Every year. Tough for a woman living without a husband," he said with a nod.

"You still a woman hater?" she asked.

"Got me an Ol' Lady now, not much older than you," he said.

"Oh shit, are you serious?" she asked as she sat in the stool beside his chair.

He crossed his arms in front of his chest and nodded his head. "Avery. Gonna get the letter "A" tattooed on my knuckle right now, kill two birds with one stone."

"I like it," she said.

"Same here," he responded as he sat down.

"You ready?" I asked.

"Ready as I'm going to get," he responded.

After wiping his arm down with soap, I shaved his bicep and began the re-work of his existing tattoo. Riley sat quietly and exchanged glances between the Axton and me as I worked. It was nice having her there watching, and being in her presence made me feel like there was a little more between us than I suspected she believed there was.

After thirty minutes, I was done with his bicep, and immediately moved to his knuckles. Ten minutes later, I was done.

"Knuckles look good," he said as he nodded his head.

"Just be careful with them. They're slow to heal with all the flexing of the skin," I said.

He gazed down at his hands, turned his head to the side and inspected his bicep, and stood from his seat.

"Good work," he said as he adjusted his vest.

I removed my gloves and tossed them in the trash. "Appreciate it."

Riley stood from her stool, walked around the end of his chair, and stopped at my side. Axton alternated glances between us for a moment.

"Oh shit, are you two…" He paused and studied Riley.

She glanced at me and shrugged her shoulder slightly.

"What, you don't know?" he asked.

I glanced toward her and grinned. "Yeah, we are."

"Yeah we are," she giggled.

"Better than your last choice, that's for sure," he said flatly.

"Yep, he hit me for the last time," she said.

Axton's cocked an eyebrow. "He what?"

"The last time he hit me, I left. Haven't seen him since," she said.

He fixed his eyes on me, held his gaze for a moment, and eventually shifted his eyes toward Riley. His mood seemed to quickly change from rather cheerful to angry almost immediately. He inhaled a deep breath, folded his arms in front of his chest, and glared.

"What was his name? *Get in a wreck, call Peck*? That's what his billboards say, right? Wasn't that it? Stephen Peck?" he asked.

She nodded her head.

He nodded his head once as he reached for his wallet.

"Here you go," he said as he handed me two one hundred dollar bills.

"Let me get you some change," I said.

"Keep it. Take her out for dinner or something. I appreciate you getting me in," he said.

"Appreciate it," I said as I shoved the bills into my pocket.

He reached down, grabbed his tee shirt, and held his right arm extended to the side. After hugging Riley and shaking my hand, he walked to his bike, started it, and left.

I turned to face Riley. "I'm guessing he didn't like that Stephen guy."

"I'm guessing not," she responded.

"Fuck, he got mad," I said.

"Uhhm, yeah. He sure seemed to."

"What are your thoughts about sleeves?" she asked.

I raised my arms in the air and twisted my wrists around slowly. "Do you really need to ask?"

"On me…" she said.

The thought of her having a sleeve excited me. Women with well thought out sleeves were almost as attractive as women with bold black-framed glasses.

Almost.

"I like the thought of it," I responded.

"Got time?" she asked.

I glanced beyond her and toward Tyler's empty work station.

"I've got a lifetime," I responded.

RILEY

I felt I had gone from being single forever to being mentally committed to Blake in a matter of two weeks. Whatever it was that drew me to him was sufficient enough for me to let my guard down, accept him as being a minimal threat, and welcome him into my life. I did realize we weren't committed in a relationship sense, but for me, it was important I viewed it as otherwise. My belief that we were much more involved than we really were allowed me to look at him in a much different light than if we were simply hanging out as friends.

"It's healing nicely," he said as he inspected my sleeve.

"I love it. I figured she'd throw a fit, but my mom loves it too," I said.

"That's good, you always want to keep your mother on your good side," he said as he released my wrist.

"So, you've never mentioned your parents. Do they live here?" I asked.

He shifted his eyes toward the door and stared blankly at the entrance, his eyes narrow and his thoughts obviously deep. "No, they don't."

I nodded my head. "Oh. How often do you…"

"They died when I was young. I grew up in an orphanage for most of my childhood, but then went to live with a foster family for a while," he said flatly.

I felt like such a fool. I didn't know anyone who was an orphan, and the thought of him being without a family made me feel sick. As I stood and tried to devise a way to console him, my eyes welled with tears and my throat began to tighten.

"I'm. I'm, uhhm, I'm sorry," I said as I reached for his shoulder.

He continued to stare out the window, squinting his eyes as if he were still in deep thought. Slowly, he raised his arm, placed his palm over my hand, and turned toward me slightly. "Yeah, me too, I wish I could change it, but I can't."

Everyone has secrets; revealing them is simply a matter of finding out where to dig. Blake hadn't shared his parent's death with me, and I guess I shouldn't have expected him to. It obviously wasn't something he intended to hide from me forever, but he more than likely hoped to hide it until he was ready to share it with me. Unknowingly, I had dug in the right spot.

Or maybe the wrong spot.

I wanted to ask how they died, but I didn't dare. From time to time I had heard on the news about a family being killed in a car wreck, or a train colliding with a car on the tracks outside of town, but I never thought to think if there was a child who wasn't with the family when it happened. I realized in the future as I heard of such events, I would wonder if there was a lone child without any other family to care for him or her, and whether or not they would become an orphan. The thought of it all began to consume me, and my stomach started to feel ill.

I turned toward him, opened my arms, and hugged him. Based on his light pat against my back with his hand, it was apparent he really didn't want to be held, so I released him. Feeling like a complete fool, I attempted to change the subject.

"So, it's almost lunchtime, want me to run and get some sandwiches?" I asked.

He turned toward me and seemed to force a smile. "Sounds good."

The sound of the door buzzer caused me to glance up. An adorable girl covered in tattoos from her wrists to the sleeves of her tee shirt walked in, glanced around the shop, and slowly walked toward the wall separating the waiting area from the shop. Dressed in brick-red jeans that were tight all the way to her ankles, a *Mr. Zoggs Sex Wax* tee shirt, and sneakers, she sure didn't look like a local. As she leaned onto the countertop, she tossed her purple-highlighted brunette hair over her shoulders. As I stood and admired her, I envied her slightly.

I shifted my eyes from her to Blake, and back to her.

"What can I do for you?" Blake asked as he approached the counter.

"Name's Stevie, and before you ask, yeah, it's my real name. Just moved here from San Diego, and I was just wondering if you need any artists. I'm licensed in California, Oregon, and maybe still in Washington. Fuck, I don't know. But anyway, are you needing any artists? I'm bad as fuck with black and grey and I specialize in new school and realism," she said.

Blake nodded his head. "Have you got a portfolio or anything?"

"Hold please," she said as she pulled her pack from her shoulder.

After a minute of digging, she produced a book. She tossed it on the counter in front of Blake.

"There you go," she said.

Blake picked up the book, flipped through the pages, and folded it closed.

"All that's yours?" he asked.

She shook her head as she reached for the book. "No, I stole the shit online and put it in there, hoping for a job. I've really been working at Jack in the Box since 2010, and I wanted a change of pace."

Blake stared.

"Yeah, it's mine. You like it?" she asked.

He nodded his head and grinned. "A thousand a month booth rent, due the first of the month, and not after. That buys your rent for the month following payment. I have an extra chair, two stools, and a drawing table back there, you're more than welcome to them."

"So, you're offering me a spot?" she asked.

Blake nodded.

"Fuck yeah!" she hollered as she thrust her hands in the air.

She raised her chin slightly and fixed her eyes on me. "You work here?"

I shook my head..

"What? She your girl?" she asked as she shifted her eyes toward Blake.

"Yeah, she is. Riley, meet Stevie," he said.

I took the few steps between Blake and me and stepped to his side. I held my hand out, and after tossing the book into her backpack, she shook my hand.

"Bad-ass piece on your arm," she said as she nodded her head toward my forearm.

I tossed my head toward Blake and wagged my eyebrows. "Thanks."

She shifted her eyes toward Blake.

"Your work?" she asked.

"Sure is," he responded.

She turned to face me, held out her open hand, and grinned. "You mind?"

"No, not at all," I said as I extended my arm.

She lightly held my wrist, inspected my arm carefully, and grinned as she released my wrist.

"Good line work. Love what you did with the shading. It's got great depth," she said.

"Appreciate it," he said.

"Like your hair," she said.

"Thanks," I responded.

"Well, come on back?" Blake asked as he motioned toward the shop.

"Sure," she responded as she grabbed her pack.

I walked to the side of the partition with no other motive other than to inspect her tattoos. As she stepped past the edge of the chest-high wall and caught a complete glimpse of me, she stopped in her tracks and widened her eyes.

"God damn. You've got a cute little ass on you, don't you?" she said.

I stood and stared, uncertain of what to say, if anything.

"Don't worry, I'm not gay and I won't attack you or anything, I'm just saying. I wish I had an ass like that," she said as she began following Blake to the rear of the shop.

"Uhhm. Thank you?" I said as she walked away.

"So, what's a girl got to do to get an ass like that?" she asked as we stopped at Tyler's old work station.

"Genetics," Blake responded.

"I uhhm. I run on the treadmill," I said.

"You run on the treadmill?" she said with a note of sarcasm.

I shrugged my shoulders. "Yeah."

"Well, I've surfed since I was six, and look at this fucker," she said as she slapped her hand against her ass.

121

"It's cute," I said.

"Not like that," she said as she leaned to the side and raised her eyebrows.

"Well, here's the spot. The stools, chair, and drawing table are yours to use, but if you leave, they stay here. I'll give you two months before you must pay rent, but when you do, back rent is due, understood?" Blake asked.

"Fuck yeah, I appreciate it. You won't regret it," she said.

"Most shops open at noon. I open at ten. Close at nine. I'll expect you here at your station when I unlock the door and here when I lock it up at night, whether you're busy or not," Blake said.

"You can bet on it," she said as she lowered her backpack to the floor.

I was tall for a girl, or at least I always thought I was. At five foot seven, there weren't many girls who were taller than me. As I studied Stevie and made note of where the top of her head was in relationship to Blake's arm, I decided she was more than likely five foot tall, and not an inch taller. She was well proportioned and had some nice curves, but she was just smaller than any other woman I had ever seen.

"I don't care what you charge hourly, as long as it's between ninety and one-thirty," Blake said.

"With this cheap rent, I won't argue. Charged one-fifty in SD," she said.

"Figures," Blake said.

"So how long have you two been together? You're a cute couple. I just can't get over your ass," she said with a laugh as she shook her head.

"Uhhm," I said.

"We've been together for a bit," Blake interrupted.

"It shows," she said nod.

Blake rubbed his hands together, something I hadn't seen in several days, or maybe even longer. After alternating glances between us for a few seconds, he fixed his eyes on Stevie and stopped with the hand thing.

"So, start tomorrow?" he asked.

"Yeah, I'll get my shit in here now if it's alright," she said.

"Okay by me," he said.

"So," Blake said as he turned to face me.

"You want to just run and get something and bring it back," he asked.

I shook my head. "No, I'll call it in. Maybe the Anchor, they deliver."

"Anchor sounds good," he said.

I liked the thought of Blake getting employees who were less abrasive than Tyler, but I wasn't one hundred percent comfortable having Stevie working with him all day every day. She was far too pretty, much too outgoing, and a little more eager than I was comfortable with. Feeling slightly jealous, a little bit like I was in a competition, and like my ass was larger than she was leading me to believe, I turned toward her and smiled.

"You probably don't eat bar food, do you?" I asked.

"I eat anything, why would you think that?" she asked.

I widened my eyes slightly and shrugged my shoulders. "I don't know, I just figured because you were so tiny, maybe you were vegan or vegetarian or something."

"So, because I don't have a nice round ass, I must eat bean sprouts or something?" she said with a laugh.

"Something like that," I responded.

"I eat anything, why?" she said.

"We were going to get something from the bar down the street, and I wondered if you wanted something. There's a menu up on the refrigerator," I said as I pointed to the rear of the shop.

"Yeah, I'll eat, thanks," she paused, raised her hand to the side of her mouth as if preparing to tell me a secret, and leaned forward.

I bent down slightly and glanced toward Blake as she continued.

"Don't worry, honey. I'm not after your man. I only fuck guys with big cocks, and then only if they ride a Harley. He doesn't have a big cock or ride a HOG does he?" she whispered.

I stood with my mouth hanging open and stared blankly at Blake.

"I'm just fucking with ya," she said as she slapped the palm of her hand against my shoulder.

I forced a shitty grin and tried to decide if she was being truthful or playing around.

"You've got nothing to worry about," she said.

"Thanks," I responded.

I watched as she unzipped her pack, dumped it on the table, and began to rifle through the contents, which were mostly sketches and books. After a few minutes, everything was in neat piles, and she walked toward the refrigerator. A quick glance at the menu, and she walked back to her work station and reached for a little black zippered bag.

"Here's twenty," she said as she handed me a twenty dollar bill. "Leave the change for a tip."

"Uhhm. What do you want?" I asked.

"Bacon cheeseburger," she said as she slapped her hand against the side of her ass. "Maybe it'll fatten me up."

I grinned, shook my head, and turned toward Blake.

"Mac and cheese and a grilled cheese," he said.

"They have grilled cheese?" Stevie asked.

"Yeah, it's good," I responded.

"No, fuck it. I want the burger. I'll get the grilled cheese next time," she said.

"Here," Blake said as he held out his hand. "Let me go get it, you can stay here and talk to Stevie."

I eagerly handed him Stevie's money. He called in the order, and after straightening up his work station, he said goodbye and walked to the bar.

"He's got a big cock, doesn't he?" she asked as soon as Blake walked out the door.

I stared at her with wide eyes, shocked that she'd ask such a question. On one hand I wanted to respond and tell her the truth, bragging about the size of his bulge. On the other hand, I wanted to say no, just to make sure she wasn't interested in pursuing him. In the end, it got down to whether or not I trusted Blake, and although he had done nothing specific to gain my trust, I had no real reason not to.

"It's huge," I said.

"I fucking knew it," she said as she held her hand in the air.

I slapped my hand against hers and grinned. "How'd you know?"

"I can tell. How he walks, how he carries himself," she said.

I nodded my head as if I knew what she was talking about even though I had no clue.

"So, why'd you move here from San Diego?" I asked.

"Got tired of being used as a punching bag," she said.

"Broke up with the ex?" I asked.

"Not so much. Left when he got tossed in jail," she said.

I nodded my head. "I left mine six months ago."

"Left your what?" she asked.

"My boyfriend beat me up too. I left him," I said.

"Fuck yes," she said as she held her hand in the air again.

I slapped her hand. "Fuck yes," I repeated.

"What brought you here?" I asked as I pointed to the floor.

"Oh here? Like Wichita?" she asked.

I nodded my head. "Yeah, here."

"My mother. I was living in California with my father through high school. So, I just stayed there. My mother lives here, so I said 'good bye, asshole', and here I am," she said.

"Well, I'm glad you're away from him," I said.

"I'll use you as my inspiration. Maybe in six months I'll be getting some of that big Kansas cock, just like you," she said.

"Maybe so," I said.

I turned toward the door as the buzzer sounded. Blake walked in carrying two bags. I glanced down at his crotch. There was an obvious bulge in the center of his jeans. It looked like he was sneaking a pickle in with the lunch he carried. I took a step back and watched him walk into the shop. With each step, his left hip twitched rearward slightly and his shoulder followed. It was something, until Stevie had mentioned it, that I had yet to notice.

He had a certain element of swagger to his walk. She was right. Blake had a big cock and he knew it.

And so did I.

Somehow I needed to convince him to let me have it.

BLAKE

My life had been a series of ups and downs, never staying in one place for very long. I did realize I played a huge part in the peaks and valleys in which my mind resided, but maintaining an even keel was difficult for me, and even though I realized it was difficult for everyone else on earth, it was apparent it wasn't *equally* difficult.

I was different.

I had always been different.

I found comfort in Riley; what she offered me mentally, physically, and emotionally was unlike anything I had previously received as the result of human contact. Keeping her in my life would require consistency on my part, and being constant or living an unchanging life had never been strengths I possessed.

Confused on how to proceed with life, but desperately wanting my time with her to continue, the answer came to me at an AA meeting. Or, at least what I believed to be the answer. Steps two, three, and four were exactly what I needed to apply to my life. I felt if I adhered to the principles of the program, progress was certain.

There was no way millions of converted drunks could be wrong.

"Came to believe that a Power greater than ourselves could restore us to sanity." This was easy for me. I had been trying to restore myself to sanity for some time, and had been rather unsuccessful. In fact, my way of doing things landed me in the very meetings I was using to attempt to correct my life. For me to believe God or a resemblance of God might be able to make changes for the better in me and my life was simple. I knew I couldn't, so to believe he could wasn't a stretch at all.

"Made a decision to turn our will and our lives over to the care of God *as we understood Him.*" If I wanted the previous step to work for me, believing this step could be skipped or cast aside was impossible. I had never been a person to pray, go to church, or even discuss God, but I was now convinced my lack of contact with him just might have contributed to the emotional roller coaster my life had become.

"Made a searching and fearless moral inventory of ourselves." After discussing the steps with an old timer, he explained the importance of performing this step. If I stepped out of myself and stood as a critical examiner of who Blake West was from a moral standpoint, I was disappointed with him. This step allowed me to become aware of the changes I needed to make in me to become the person I deeply desired to be.

But first things should always come first, so I prayed for the ability to have eyes that could see, ears that could hear, and a mind that was able to discern right from wrong.

I was now proceeding with life listening more, talking less, and at least attempting to be a man with a moral compass. As much as I admired Riley and her simple way of living life, I decided to follow her lead. I expected if I did, my life would become a mirror image of hers.

Or so I hoped.

"The food was fantastic," I said as I leaned away from the table.

"Thank you," Riley's mother said. "I can't take complete credit, Riley helped out."

"Well, to whoever was in involved, it was fabulous," I said.

They looked at each other and shared a moment of infectious pride. Riley's mother wasn't at all what I expected her to be. I envisioned a slightly overweight housewife wearing an apron covered in flour and handprints, having her hair pinned in neat little sections - always one step away from finishing it. Through the house she would run, trying desperately to have the meal prepared in time, later apologizing for her appearance as we ate.

From twenty feet away, she could pass for Riley. Sitting side by side, they could easily pass for sisters who were ten years apart in age. She shared Riley's lips, eyes, facial structure, and body. And, although I wasn't sexually attracted to Riley's mother, noticing she also shared Riley's little round ass was painfully obvious.

"So, what made you decide to become a tattoo artist?" her mother asked.

I stared down at my forearm and recalled my first tattoo. The piece was on my chest; something I intended to hide from everyone but felt I desperately needed to make my life complete. A traditional tattoo - a dagger through a skull - represented bravery to me. Receiving the tattoo was a huge step, something I wanted to do for a long time but had always found a reason not to get. One day when the time was right I went into a tattoo parlor, tossed the money on the counter, and let the artist proceed at will.

The remaining tattoos were like everything else in my life, the result of an addict feeding his addictions. I didn't regret any of them, as I felt the combination of all of my artwork in some way, shape, or form depicted who I was - or at least who I was at the time I received them.

In all honesty, the tattoos changed me. Receiving each one allowed me to release something from within myself I had spent a lifetime either subconsciously protecting, or attempting to rid myself of.

But.

It was the artist that made each and every one of them possible.

I shifted my eyes from my forearm to Riley's mother and did my best to explain myself. "Tattooing in the United States started in the 1800's, and the first tattoo parlor opened in New York City in 1870. A German immigrant who had spent his time in the states tattooing Civil War soldiers finally decided to open a shop offering his service to anyone willing to spend the money to get a tattoo. In 1891, a man invented the electric tattoo machine, and tattooing really took off."

I opened my arms wide and leaned toward the table. "Tattoos have become a way for people to represent bravery, receive perceived protection, or in remembrance of an event or person. For many, myself included, they're an outlet - but they are always permanent, and they're only as good as the man who applies them; the artist. I had always been a great artist and took tremendous pride in my work, so I decided to offer the service of changing the lives of people one tattoo at a time. I believe the quality of my work is second to no one. The sad thing is most people won't even realize it until a decade or two has passed, and their brother's, sister's, or friend's tattoos are awful looking while theirs are still as good as day one. So, I don't know, I think I started because I wanted to make a difference in people's lives."

I leaned back in my chair and waited for the arguments to start.

"That's an admirable reason. I've always wanted one, but was afraid it would hurt too much. Does it hurt?" she asked.

"It does. Anyone who says it doesn't is lying. It's the price you pay in addition to the price you pay. A tattoo is a huge commitment, and the pain is part of the commitment, I suppose," I said.

"I'll wait until I'm ready," she said.

Riley turned toward her mother and widened her eyes slightly. "I didn't know you wanted a tattoo."

"I've always wanted one. Well, not always, but for a long time," she responded.

"Of what?" Riley asked.

"That's just it," her mother said. "I don't know."

"So, you've never been married, and you don't have any children?" she asked.

I pursed my lips and shook my head from side-to-side. "No ma'am. No ex-wives, no kids."

"And no family. I'm sorry," she said.

"Don't be sorry. It's not your fault. I've got Riley, she's family enough," I said.

I turned toward Riley and smiled. She smiled in return. She looked even more beautiful than normal, I guessed as the result of being filled with the pride from having me meet her mother. Regardless of the reason, she was beautiful beyond compare.

In the past, I had likened a beautiful woman to a beautiful tattoo; something that took care and imagination to develop, yet required constant maintenance to prolong the elegance.

Riley was an exception. She was beautiful without preparation or maintenance.

"I'm going to get the sweets," Riley said as she stood from her seat.

I pushed myself from the table and stood. "Let me help."

"No, I'll get it. You can sit and talk," she said as she turned away.

Riley disappeared into the kitchen, leaving me alone with her mother. For whatever reason, being alone with her caused me to be slightly uncomfortable. I had no reason, and although I wasn't sure, I suspected being around Riley's mother caused me to understand I didn't have a mother, at least not one that was alive.

She leaned forward and studied me for a short time, making me even more nervous. After what seemed like an eternity, but couldn't have been more than ten seconds, she sighed lightly.

"So, your name is Blake, you don't have kids, you've never been married, and you're nice to my daughter, at least from what she says. You have manners, you're well spoken, and you have your own business. In my mind, Riley hit a home run. Have you always lived here?" she asked.

"Yes ma'am," I responded.

"If I may ask, what's your last name?" she asked.

"West," I said.

"Blake West?" she asked.

I nodded my head. "Yes ma'am."

She shifted her eyes to the side and sat quietly as she appeared to become lost in thought. As I sat nervously waiting for her to continue, she didn't. After a moment, Riley came into the room carrying a platter with coffee and slices of cake.

"Tiramisu, your favorite," she said as she held the platter in front of me.

I reached for a cup of coffee and a slice of cake. "My favorite?"

"No," she said. "Hers."

"Riley, I'm sorry," her mother said as she stood. "Blake, my apologies. I'm going to have to go to my room. I'm afraid my stomach has gone sick, like bad sick."

"Mom, are you okay?" Riley asked.

Her mother shook her head. She appeared totally different than she had all night. Instead of the cheerful woman who we had shared dinner with, her face appeared vacant and lost.

"I'm sorry Riley. I'm afraid I'm going to be sick," she said as she raised her hand to her mouth.

"Blake," she said as she turned to face me. "It was a pleasure."

I stood from my seat and nodded my head. "Thank you ma'am. Likewise."

"I'm sorry, mom," Riley said.

Her mother nodded, forced herself to smile, turned and walked away. In a few steps she disappeared down the hallway which led into the living area of the house.

"That's sad. I was having fun. What happened?" Riley asked.

"I was too. I don't know. We were talking and she seemed to fade away or something. Does she do that?" I asked.

"What do you mean?" she asked as she lowered the platter to the table.

As she sat down, I continued. "I don't know. She told me she thought you hit a home run in finding me then she asked me my last name. I answered her and she looked like she was trying to think of something else to ask, and she just faded off. Like her eyes got glazed over and glassy and she didn't say anything else. Then you walked in."

"Huh. No, she doesn't do anything like that. Maybe it was the chicken or something. I thought it was cooked all the way through. Do you feel okay?" she asked.

I raised my cup of coffee. "I'm good."

She tilted her head toward the cup. "Black, just like you like it."

"Thanks," I said as I took a sip of the much needed coffee.

"Wow. Well, that sucks," she said as she tilted her head toward the hallway.

"Yeah, bad deal," I said as I sipped the coffee.

We sat and ate the three pieces of cake, sharing the third piece. The differences in doing what we were doing and what I was accustomed to doing were drastic. Sitting in the shop eating a sandwich left over from lunch at ten o'clock at night was my typical dinner a month before I met Riley, and now I was eating tiramisu with a fork and drinking coffee from an ornate porcelain cup.

I glanced at her and grinned, truly grateful for her allowing me into her life.

"Let me clean this up and we'll go back to my room," she said as she stood from her seat.

"Your room? You don't live here," I said.

She scrunched her nose and stared. "I used to. When I left my room didn't disappear."

"Oh," I said as I stood.

Together we carried the dishes to the kitchen, loaded the dishwasher, and cleaned the countertops and the dining room table. After everything was back to the way it was long before our arrival, she held her hand to the side and shifted her eyes in my direction.

I encompassed her hand in mine as I followed her out of the kitchen and along the same hallway her mother had disappeared down. The last door on the left was open, revealing a perfectly preserved bedroom from when I expected Riley left immediately following high school.

"It's bright," I said as I peered through the door.

She tugged against my arm. "Come on."

After she pulled my arm straight, I shuffled behind her and into the room. The bed was covered in a pale yellow comforter and decorated with no less than a dozen pillows - all a different shade of yellow or blue. Two of the walls were painted light grey, and the other two were painted a complimentary blue-grey.

Although it certainly wouldn't have been my choice of colors, it looked like she had hired someone to decorate it. For a normal person to choose the colors of all of the accessories in the room and have them match as well as they did would have been impossible.

"Did your mom hire someone to do this?" I asked as I gazed around the room.

"Do what?" she asked.

"Decorate this room."

"No," she said. "I did it myself. Like it?"

I nodded my head and turned to face her. "It looks really good."

She swept her arm across the bed, clearing it of almost all of the pillows in one swipe. After tossing a few loose pillows into the pile, two were left on the bed.

"Sit," she said as she walked toward the dresser.

Soft jazz began to fill the room.

"I used to listen to that CD every night when I went to sleep. It was like my lullaby," she said.

"Soothing," I said.

She sat on the edge of the bed and patted the comforter with her hand. "Sit."

Reluctantly, I kicked off my shoes and sat down on the edge of the bed.

"Uhhm. I'm really glad you came over. My mother likes you. I knew she would, but it's nice to see her happy," she said as she rested her hand on my thigh.

"I'm glad I came, too," I said as I glanced down at her hand.

Although Riley and I had been seeing each other for almost a month, we had yet to make any progress from a sexual standpoint. When the time came, and as long as I was ready, I figured I would allow myself to proceed sexually with her. Her actions, words, and constant innuendoes were enough for me to understand she was more than ready, but it was me I was worried about.

And for good reason.

"Blake," she said as she squeezed my thigh in her hand lightly.

I continued to glance around the room as I responded. "Yeah?"

"I uhhm…I want to…I want to. I want to give you head," she said.

"Excuse me?"

"I want to make you happy," she said.

She had caught me completely off guard. "I am happy," I said, providing a rather feeble statement to assure her I was.

"I want to do this," she said as she leaned toward me and kissed me lightly.

I felt my cock rising in my pants as my mind floated away to thoughts of her lips wrapping around the shaft of my rod. As I attempted to clear my mind of the thought, she began to fumble with my belt and zipper.

No differently than men who get coerced into robbing a bank, committing murder, or buying a new car they had only hoped to test drive, I sat and stared as she pulled my pants to mid-thigh. My boxers soon followed, and as much as I believed I wanted her to stop, I provided absolutely no effort to make her do so. Within a matter of sixty seconds, she had my cock in her hand and gazed down at it admiringly.

"Your cock is pretty," she said.

I swallowed and had every intention of saying something.

But nothing came.

I watched in slight shock and utter amazement as she licked the tip, dragged her tongue along the shaft, and eventually softly began to suck the swollen head in her mouth.

As I continued to stare no differently than the deer immediately prior to catching the front bumper of a truck on the highway, she slowly worked her mouth up and down the shaft of my swollen dick.

A combination of who she was, how I felt about her, and witnessing what she was doing aroused me to a level I had yet to know. Her sheer beauty alone was enough to put me over the edge and leave me with very little, if any, stamina.

Realizing she chose to do what she was doing with no suggestion or comment on my part was enough in itself to convince me she truly cared for me and wanted to share herself with me in a more intimate sense than a simple friendly relationship of kissing, holding hands, and talking. As odd as it seemed to accept, her sucking my cock was the deciding factor in me falling over the edge of the cliff into the abyss known as love that lingered below.

As I felt my heartbeat increase and my blood pressure begin to rise, I reached for her head. Despite my halfhearted attempts to pull her mouth free of the fleshy shaft she was determined to impale herself on, she continued without breaking her rhythm. I proceeded to watch in a combination of amazement and admiration as she worked her mouth and hand simultaneously along the length of my throbbing rod.

With her eyes locked on mine and her mouth full of cock, she pressed her lips lower and lower, eventually coughing warm slobber onto my tight scrotum. Lost in a state of sexual awe, my toes curled, my head tilted back, and in a matter of seconds, I erupted into her warm wet mouth.

And the world didn't end.

What in many respects seemed like a lifetime, even knowing it was more than likely a matter of a few short minutes, had ended peacefully and without any harm. I lowered myself to the bed, rested on my back, and gazed upward. Her head soon came to rest on my stomach, and after studying the brush strokes in the paint on the ceiling for a considerable time, I rolled my head to the side and allowed myself the pleasure of seeing her.

She blinked her eyes and grinned.

"Did you enjoy it," she asked.

I grinned. The grin soon developed into a full-fledged smile. "Do you need to ask?"

"No, but it's nice to hear," she said.

"It felt wonderful," I responded.

"Good. I like that you liked it," she said.

I shook my head, still smiling from ear to ear. "No, I loved it."

She nestled her head into my stomach. I relaxed on my back with one hand resting on her shoulder and the other on her neck. Cradling her head against me was comforting, and within a short period of time I fell asleep.

***

I shook Riley's shoulder. She turned to the side, opened her eyes slightly, and grinned.

"I need to get home," I said. "It's three in the morning."

"Just stay," she said, her raspy voice proof of the fact she was exhausted.

"I don't think your mother would approve, and it'd make me uncomfortable if I did. Some other time, okay?" I said.

"Okay," she said.

I leaned down and kissed her lightly on the lips, wishing I could stay, but fully realizing it was in our best interest if I didn't.

"I'll lock the door," I said as I turned away.

She opened her eyes slightly and grinned again. "Okay."

And although I realized I would never understand why our hearts and minds do what they do when they choose to do it, I walked through the door and to my motorcycle fully realizing that somehow, while I slept with her at my side, I had somehow fallen in love with Riley Campbell.

RILEY

I opened the door slightly and peeked into my mother's room. On the floor was a small cardboard box, and surrounding it were numerous pieces of paper which from where I was standing seemed to be old faded newspaper articles. I shifted my eyes to her bed. She appeared to be asleep.

I pushed the door open a little more.

"Mother?" I said softly.

Curious of what it was she had spread around the floor, and being careful not to wake her, I walked into the room softly, hoping to at least get an idea of what it was she had been doing.

It didn't take long.

One article positioned beside the box immediately caught my attention based solely on the word "murder" being in the headline. I glanced at her, made note of her snoring, and reached for the article. As I raised it high enough that the small black print was legible, I fought to keep quiet.

Recent Murder Tied to Previous Murders

An east Wichita couple murdered during broad daylight last month has been officially linked by the Police Commissioner to a series of previously unsolved murders based on the modus operandi.

The commissioner gave few details regarding the investigation in the murder of Brandon and Velma West, which left their six year old son a ward of the state, but did agree to a press conference regarding the previous murders, which is now scheduled for Tuesday...

Feeling confused, almost sick, and curious at the same time, I carefully placed the article back where it was. If the people in the article were Blake's parents, I wondered why my mother would have clipped the section of newspaper and kept it for so many years. As I mentally dismissed it to her simply keeping track of the investigation of a local psychopath long since deceased or imprisoned, I noticed another article at the foot of her bed. I tilted my head to the side and gazed down at the article.

Survivor's Testimony Convicts Serial Killer

According to the prosecution team, Jaye Campbell's testimony was paramount in the conviction of Ted Wayne Mastick in the murder of her husband, Jonathon. Assistant District Attorney Nelda Freemont shared her belief with Wichita Eagle reporter Tom Whiteside that the trial was destined to be a mistrial until Mrs. Campbell came forward immediately prior to the selection of jurors.

With her throat cut and left for dead, Mrs. Campbell walked to a neighbor's home and calmly asked to use the phone after realizing her phone lines had been severed during the invasion of her home...

I began to sob.

Apparently, my father had not been killed in a car wreck, and my mother's scar wasn't the result of a glass shard. Within seconds my mother was up on her feet attempting to comfort me.

"Why...what...I can't...even think," I blubbered.

"Riley, please. Listen..."

"To what," I shouted. "Another lie?"

"Riley," she said as she wrapped her arms around me. "I couldn't tell you the truth. I just couldn't. I was trying to protect you."

"From…from what?" I asked as I pushed her away.

"From being hurt," she said.

Now a full-blown sobbing mess, I stood with my hands against my thighs and cried, heaving to find my next breath. She leaned over, wrapped her arm around my shoulder, and held me against her side.

"When you're a mother, you'll understand," she said. "You will. Everything I told you was true. Your father and I were in an accident, he died, and my throat was cut and I ended up in the hospital. All I failed to tell you was the truth about what exactly the accident was."

"He was…he was murdered," I blubbered.

She was much calmer than I was comfortable with. As I continued to fight for my next breath, she stood and held me. I guessed she had a few decades of time to come to terms with what happened, and I had only had a few minutes. As she patted her hand against my back, I remembered what I had read about the West family.

I turned my head to the side and glanced up and into her eyes. "And Blake. Were they…were they his…"

She nodded her head. "Those were his parents mentioned in the article, yes."

I bit my lower lip to prevent it from quivering.

"What…why…How did you know?"

"Last night, when he told me his name…" She paused and inhaled a deep breath. After a long sigh, she continued. "I figured out he was the orphan from that murder. After what happened to your father and me, I became obsessed with the case for a while. It was my way of letting go. Riley, I'm so sorry."

143

I tried to stand, couldn't, and continued to lean against my thighs. My mother pulled me to the edge of the bed and helped me sit. As I sat with my face in my hands, she continued to explain.

She began to speak in a soft comforting tone without much emotion at all. As she spoke, I did my best to listen, and hoped to understand why she did what she did.

"That man killed people here for a long, long time. I testified against him in court. I put him away, Riley. It was harder than you might think, and setting that part of my life aside would have never happened if you knew the truth about what I had gone through. Forgetting it would have been - and still is - impossible, but even functioning with a daily reminder of what happened would have crushed us both. I felt if I told you the truth you'd go through all of the pain and hardship I went through, and I just couldn't do that to you. All I wanted was what was best for you," she said.

It wasn't difficult for me to understand how much pain she had gone through. Just with my experiences with Stephen, I suffered greatly. She was right. For her to share what happened with me as a child, my life would have been totally different.

And, for me to understand what life would have been like knowing would have been impossible. As I turned to give her a hug, I hoped deep in my heart that Blake had no idea of what happened to his parents. I hoped somehow he escaped the truth no differently than I had.

"I love you," I said as I wrapped my arms around her.

"I love you so much," she said as she held me in her arms.

As we sat on the edge of the bed and held each other, I realized everything she had done she did with the hope of preventing me from being hurt. She realized the pain I would go through based on the pain she had felt.

Ultimately, my mother was protecting me from harm.

And I loved her even more for doing so.

BLAKE

I had felt for the last month that Riley and I were making progress and working toward a meaningful relationship, but hadn't really felt the relationship was solid until the previous night in her room. Now praying Mr. Racine didn't press the subject, I hoped to be in and out without any problems or red flags.

"The meetings, Mr. West. Let's talk about the meetings," he said.

"Progress, not perfection. That's what they teach us, and that's what I'm practicing. I'm making progress. Next subject, please," I said.

"No, we're going to discuss them and what your expectations are surrounding the meetings," he said.

"Fucking whatever. You ask, I'll answer," I said.

As he scribbled on his pad I began to pick at the sole of my shoe.

"Alright. We have both agreed your problems with drinking spawned the desire to attempt another approach at life, and the meetings were a proven method for many people to stop drinking." He paused and glared at me.

I tossed my hands in the air. "What?"

"I'd prefer that you pay attention," he said.

I glanced up from my shoe. "Drinking spawned meetings. Meetings are good for many people. I'm a multitasker, Mr. Racine. Continue."

He tapped the pen against his lip, eventually stopped, and allowed it to dangle loosely from between his thumb and forefinger. "Very well. Now, what I would like for you to discuss is why you feel a need or necessity to utilize the meetings as a stepping stone to recover from an addiction to sex and drugs when neither have been of concern. Can you expand on your thought process?"

"What are you talking about?" I asked.

"Mr. West. Unless something has happened I am unaware of, you aren't nor have you ever been sexually active," he paused and raised the pen to his lip.

"What's your point?" I asked.

"Mr. West. Your application of the principles of the twelve step program to recover from sex addiction is without merit. We discussed this briefly six weeks ago, and you refused to discuss it in the last meeting, choosing to storm out and..." he paused and flipped through his notes.

He studied the pad of paper for a moment and eventually glanced upward. "Demand that I refer to you as 'Brainiac' upon your return."

"Okay. Are you going to make a point?" I asked.

"My point is this. You've suffered from grandiose delusional disorder in the past, and it appears you're suffering from it again," he said.

"I'm good," I said.

"Are you of the opinion you're a sex addict?" he asked.

I shook my head, "Nope."

He nodded his head and pressed the tip of the pen to the pad. After writing for a moment, he shifted his gaze upward and locked his eyes on mine. "And why aren't you of that opinion?"

"Never had sex before," I said.

"So, you haven't had problems in the past with having sex with your clients?" he asked.

I shook my head from side-to-side. "Nope."

He scribbled on the pad for a moment, paused, and then continued scribbling. After exhausting himself and flipping to one more new sheet of paper, he placed the pen beside the pad and nodded his head.

"Have you had the urge to drink?" he asked.

"Well, no shit, Doc. I'm a fucking alcoholic. I want to drink right now. I want to drink when I wake up. Before I go to bed. Hell, I wish I had a beer to drink while I'm taking a shit. Yeah, I got an urge, but I'm not acting on it," I said.

"Very well. Have you seen improvements in your life since you've chosen to abstain?" he asked.

"Yeah. Big ones. I met the girl. And, we're sexually active," I said.

He cocked an eyebrow.

"No, really. We are," I said.

"And how does that cause you to feel?" he asked.

I shrugged my shoulders. "Okay, I suppose."

"Any problems with repressed memories or flashbacks?" he asked.

I shook my head. "No. I mean I remember all that shit, but it doesn't bother me so much. I mean it does and it doesn't."

"Can you explain further?" he asked.

I shrugged my shoulders. "Well I went to her mother's house and met her mom and everything the other night, and after we were done eating her mom got sick and left and then she gave me head in her old bedroom. Riley, not her mom. Just to clarify."

"Oh, and it was awesome," I said.

"The memories, Mr. West., explain the memories," he said.

"Oh. What about them?" I asked.

"You said the memories do and don't bother you. Until you rid yourself of the cross, Mr. West, I fear you'll have a difficult time ridding yourself of the feelings. Would you like to explain your thoughts?" he asked.

I shook my head. "There's nothing to explain. You know what happened. If it happened to you, would you want to sit and think about it?"

"We're not talking about me, Mr. West. We're talking about you."

"The fuck we are. I'm talking about you right now. That's what I'm talking about, you. What would *you* think about it? You know, if it happened to you? Would you feel good or bad when you thought about it?" I asked.

"It didn't happen to me, Mr. West. It happened to you. Now, would you like to talk about how the memories make you feel?" he asked.

"Nope," I said.

"Very well. The sexual act. Did the act bother you or was it pleasurable?"

"Pleasurable," I said.

"During the act were there any periods of flashback or thoughts of the past?" he asked.

"No, not really," I said.

"I see. Have you any fear if you continue there may be?" he asked.

"May be what?"

"If you continue sexual activities have you any fear there may be flashbacks or recurring memories?" he asked.

"I think I'm good," I said as I glanced at the clock.

"Based on…"

I sat and glared at him. I was done talking, and all I needed to do was make it another ten minutes and I could leave.

"You believe 'you're good' based on what, Mr. West?" he asked.

"Based on the fact I believe I control that shit. You know it doesn't come from outer fucking space, it comes from my brain," I said.

"So, you're in control?"

"Yeah, I'm thinking so," I said with a nod.

"So, the belief of sexual addiction. Were you in control of that?" he asked.

I nodded my head. "Well, if you want my opinion, I created it to keep from being sexually active because I either had fear of the old memories or because I didn't want to hurt anyone. You know. Sex has always been off limits to me, and short of whacking off I've always avoided it."

"And your stories of sexual exploitations?" he asked.

"You know what they were," I said.

"I believe I do. Do you?" he asked.

"Sure," I said.

"Care to explain?" he asked.

I glanced at the clock. It was nine o'clock and I needed to get to work. I stood from my seat, cracked my knuckles, and popped my neck.

"Sure thing Doc," I said as I walked across his office.

I opened the door and turned to face him. "They were stories I made up in my head that never happened. I think my subconscious wanted an excuse to avoid sex because I was afraid of it. Well, now I'm not afraid. See you in two weeks."

"Mr. West. One more thing," he said as he raised his hand in the air. .

"Sure, I'm in a good mood," I said. "What you got?"

"Are you going to be honest with your female companion and let her know you're a virgin?" he asked.

"Not planning on being a virgin for long, Doc. See ya in two weeks," I said.

And I walked out the door.

RILEY

At eighteen years old, we're provided with the label of an adult, but being an adult at an early age requires making adult-like decisions. I sat three years beyond my declaration of reaching adulthood and watched Blake eat his sandwich convinced I didn't ever want to be an adult.

I preferred to live the remaining portion of my life not dealing with the decisions and complexities associated with being an adult. Remaining a little girl forever would allow me to live a life without complications, responsibilities, or making decisions which were potentially life-altering.

Yet.

It was time I acted as an adult.

"How is it?" I asked.

With a mouth full of food and a combination of vinegar and oil running down his forearms, he raised the sandwich in the air slightly and continued to chew.

"Good," he said over the mouthful of food.

He nodded his head toward my sandwich. I glanced down. I hadn't so much as touched my food. I reluctantly reached down and picked up the hoagie, feeling if I didn't at least eat a portion of it we would probably end up in an argument of some sort.

"Good call on the sandwich. This bread is soft as fuck," he said as he wiped the oil from his arms with a napkin.

"I like this place," I said.

"Not hungry?" he asked as he tilted his head toward my plate.

I shook my head and lowered my sandwich to my plate. "My stomach's upset a little bit."

"Well, it's not something you ate, because you haven't eaten yet today. Maybe 'cause you need to eat," he said.

I shrugged and picked up the sandwich. "Maybe."

I wanted to find out what he knew about the murders, and if he knew nothing, I preferred to be the one to tell him what happened. I had tried to place myself in his shoes and consider if he had told me what happened to my parents, and consider how I would have felt hearing the news from him. My belief of the sadness and rejection which would have followed is what prevented me from proceeding to tell him so far.

But I felt I needed to.

For us both.

The thought of us being in a meaningful relationship and me keeping secrets from him was impossible for me to process as a necessity. I sat watching him finish his lunch knowing at some point I would have to tell him something, and allow the morsel of information to lead into a conversation revealing everything I knew about his parent's death.

When was the question.

I tore the sandwich in two, took a bite from one half, and placed the pieces on my plate. After studying them for long enough to convince myself it looked like I had eaten much more than I actually had, I shifted my eyes to Blake.

"Can we go sit somewhere when we get done?" I asked.

He shrugged his shoulders. "Sure, where are you thinking?"

"I don't know," I said. "Maybe like a park or the Waterfront by the lake or something."

"Somewhere peaceful," he said.

I nodded my head. "Yeah."

"Sure. You gonna eat that?" he asked as he motioned toward my plate.

"I don't think so," I said. "My stomach still feels icky."

He reached for my plate and picked up the half of the sandwich I had taken a bite of. I grinned at the thought of him choosing it over the uneaten half. As he proceeded to devour the sandwich I realized just how simply he lived his life. Had I not asked about his parents, I was convinced he would have never mentioned them. Had I never asked about the toolbox on the sidewalk, he may have never mentioned Tyler again.

Blake was different.

As he wiped his mouth with a napkin and checked his fingers for residual matter, I ran through potential scenarios in my head of how to propose what I had learned of his parent's death. Upon deciding I would simply proceed with whatever felt best, I picked up the remaining half of the sandwich and took a small bite.

"I'm just goofing around," I said. "You ready?"

He nodded his head and stood. "Sure you don't want that?"

"No, I'm really not hungry," I responded.

After paying for the food and walking out to the motorcycle, we rode six blocks to the Waterfront, an outdoor mall which had been developed around a lake. The lake had several benches and a walking path, and I hoped I felt more comfortable talking once we sat down and relaxed together.

We walked half way around the lake hand in hand, and eventually chose a bench on the far side of the lake. As he gazed out at the body of water, he crossed his arms, sighed, and sat down.

"This is peaceful," he said.

"It is," I said as I sat down beside him.

In comparing the Blake I met to the Blake sitting on the bench, the differences could almost be described as drastic. When we met, he was fidgety and nervous acting. Now, he sat quietly and gazed out at the lake, seemingly at peace with life and everything around him.

"I like it when I think about us," I said.

He continued to gaze out at the lake. "You mean like us as a couple?"

"Yeah. Like *us*. You and me together," I said.

"Yeah, me too," he responded.

"You know.." I said, pausing as I realized I was speaking much sooner than I was prepared to.

He turned his head to the side. "What?"

"Uhhm. Well, I wanted to talk about secrets. Like maybe not secrets in a secretive sense, but things we should share with each other. Maybe something we want each other to know eventually, and are kind of like scared to say. I think we should take an opportunity to do it now," I said.

"Okay, you go first," he said.

It was going to be tough to do, but I decided if I told him the truth about my father, it may prompt him to tell me about his parents, as long as he knew what happened. I inhaled slowly, stared out at the lake, and exhaled.

"For my entire life, I thought my father was killed in a car accident," I said.

The words came much easier than I had expected. After glancing at

Blake and confirming I had his full attention, I continued.

"But I found out yesterday that all this time my mother was protecting me from what really happened. She didn't want to tell me because she was afraid it would have hurt me more. I'm glad I know now, but she was right," I said.

With his eyes filled with concern, and his hands clasped together in his lap, he inhaled a shallow breath and spoke.

"What happened?" he asked.

"He was murdered. The guy came in our house, killed my dad, and tried to uhhm…he tried to kill…" I glanced up at the sky and took a shallow breath.

"He tried to kill my mom, but uhhm…she…well, she lived. She walked to the neighbor's, called the police, and then she uhhm…she testified against him. You know, in court. He got eight life sentences after they tied him to a string of murders over something like twenty years. It's why she has that scar." I pointed to my neck. "You know, on her neck."

"I'm sorry," he said as he lifted his arm over my shoulder.

"It's okay," I said as I leaned into him. "It happened a long time ago."

It felt good to tell him the truth. It was easier than I thought, and I felt tremendous relief knowing there was really nothing about me or my past that Blake didn't know; short of the fact I knew about his parents. After he held me for a moment, he released me, leaned into the edge of the chair, and turned to face me.

"I really hate even saying anything after you said what you said, but I guess I will," he said.

"It's okay. Whatever you have to say, say it. I'm okay, really," I said as I wiped my eyes with the tip of my finger.

"I uhhm. I was an orphan. I lived with this preacher. He uhhm, he adopted a few kids, and he had some others he kept in foster care, but he didn't adopt them. I was one of the kids he didn't adopt. But uhhm." He shifted his eyes from me and gazed blankly out at the lake.

After several seconds of silence, he stood, crossed his arms, and continued to speak, but focused on the lake the entire time.

"He wasn't...uhhm...he didn't...yeah, he didn't treat us all the same. He uhhm. He had his own...his own kids. There were boys... some boys. He uhhm. He took me one day..." he paused and bit his lower lip.

I didn't like the way I was feeling. The thought of someone hurting Blake, especially as a child, wasn't something I wanted to try and understand. As I sat and fidgeted in my seat, he chewed his lower lip and continued.

"It was a Tuesday. I was eight. He and his son...you know...they uhhm. They molested me. It happened...more...uhhm. More than once. The cross I wear? I took it from his home. It's the only thing I've ever stolen. I felt like it had some special power or something, I don't know. I just knew he took something from me, and I wanted to take something from him. So I buried it in the yard. When I finally left the foster home, I took it with me. Wear it every day now."

He turned to face me and shrugged his shoulders.

"I'm so sorry," I said as I stood.

He raised his hand in the air between us. "I'm uhhm. I'm not done."

"Okay," I said.

I sat down, crossed my legs, and folded my hands in my lap. Feeling sorry for Blake, angry at his foster father, and disgusted with the system for allowing people to adopt children and not take proper care of them, I realized Blake's parents being murdered was the start of it all. In the grand scheme of things it really didn't matter what started it, but for some reason, it mattered to me.

He turned toward the lake and continued. "So...I've uhhm. I've created a safe place for my mind because of all of it. I kind of developed a subconscious fantasy or something. It...I...it's just...I'm..."

He turned to face me. "I'm a virgin."

I sat and stared, shocked almost more by what he said than I was when I read the newspaper article in my mother's room about my father. It made sense now. His running away, his reluctance to proceed sexually, and his constant excuses for needing to leave when things got heated between us.

"I'm really sorry about what happened when you were young. I hate people sometimes. Have you like...have you talked to anyone? You know, like a professional? I asked.

He nodded his head. "I see a guy."

"Like a doctor?" I asked as I stood.

"Yeah, a doctor," he said.

I opened my arms and hugged him. As we stood holding each other his breathing changed from labored to shallow. After a few more seconds, he relaxed into my arms and sighed.

"That wasn't as hard as I thought it would be," he said.

"Mine neither," I said.

"I've got one more," he said as he pulled away.

"Okay," I said.

He pointed to the bench. I sat, crossed my legs, clasped my hands together again, and waited. After he inhaled a deep breath he tilted his head back, exhaled, and turned toward me. "My parents were murdered too."

I waited for more.

He raised his eyebrows. "Nothing? No comment?"

I twisted my mouth to the side and nibbled on my lip. "Uhhm. Yeah. They were. Your parents were murdered by the same guy that murdered mine."

His face washed with wonder.

"What…why…why would you think that?" he asked.

He stumbled backward and sat down at the end of the bench. As he gazed at me with confused eyes, I explained.

"When you were over for dinner, mom said she was sick. She wasn't. After what happened to her and my dad, she said she became uhhm… like obsessed with the…you know, with the killer. She felt she needed closure. So she collected all of the old articles from the newspaper and kept them in a box." I paused and turned my palms upward.

"She recognized your last name, realized your parents were both dead, and went to her room and got down the box. She must have fallen asleep while she was going through everything. After you left, I went to check on her, thinking she was sick. I found the article. Brandon and Velma. Was that their names?" I asked.

As he nodded his head slowly, his eyes welled with tears. I spread my arms wide as my eyes did the same.

We scooted toward one another, met in the middle of the bench, and collapsed into each other's arms.

And we both shed tears we had spent a lifetime reserving for just that moment.

BLAKE

Growth. I felt that I had grown more during the last week than I had in the previous decade altogether. My expected reaction of a woman when she found out about my virginity caused me to conceal it as if it were a crime.

Riley's acknowledgement of it, her acceptance of me, and the strange bond we developed as a result of our similar losses by the hand of a murderous psychopath allowed us to be open and honest with each other completely. I felt as if I could be not only honest with her, but for the first time in my life, I was able to be honest with myself.

Stevie coughed a laugh. "What? *Natural born killer*? You're fucking kidding, right?"

The guy she was taking to was roughly five foot ten, weighed about a hundred and fifty pounds, and was wearing a wife beater, boots and jeans. His arms were covered in a variety of tattoos, most of which appeared to be done in the comfort of his home by one of his drunken friends.

He shrugged his shoulders and glared at her. "No, I'm serious," he said.

"I don't tattoo words on people. And, I don't tattoo idiots," she said. "So you're clearly double fucked."

He folded his arms in front of his chest and did his best to flex what little muscles he had on his biceps. "What are you trying to say?"

"I didn't stutter, asshole. I didn't *try* and say shit. I said it. Go somewhere else," she said as she pointed toward the door.

Riley swiveled in her stool, glanced in my direction, and raised her eyebrows. I shrugged my shoulders and grinned. If I had learned anything about Stevie in the last few weeks, it was that she didn't pull any punches, and she wasn't really afraid of anything or anyone.

"So you won't do it?" he asked.

She crossed her arms - clearly to mimic him - leaned back, and shook her head lightly. Wearing faded jeans, lace up boots, and a black wife beater, she resembled him in dress to some degree. She had proven herself to be a fabulous artist, but the entertainment value of having her in the shop made hiring her well worth it regardless of her abilities.

"How many people have you killed?" she asked flatly.

"None of your business," he responded.

"Kill somebody real quick, and I'll do it. I've never done a single piece of script, but if you'll kill somebody real quick, you know, show me you're a killer, fuck it, I'll do it," she said.

His eyes widened and his mouth fell open. "Are you fucking serious?"

"Yeah," she said as she pulled her knife from her back pocket and held it at arm's length.

"Kill her. Or him. Fuck it, kill 'em both," she said as she shook the knife in front of him.

She extended her left arm and wagged her index finger at Riley.

He turned his head toward Riley, made eye contact for a moment, and quickly turned to face Stevie. Riley's eyes stayed fixed on Stevie as they narrowed slightly. Although the conversation was regarding something as serious as killing, I fought to keep from laughing.

He scrunched his nose and glared at Stevie. "I can't do that," he said.

"Yeah, no shit. Beat feet, dumbass," she said as she slid the knife into her back pocket.

"Fucking bitch," he said as he turned away.

"Excuse me?" she said as she reached for her knife again.

I raised my index finger, caught her attention, and shook my head from side-to-side. As she released the knife, she gazed down at the floor and sighed. He glanced over his shoulder, coughed a laugh, and continued to walk toward the door.

Stevie shook her head, exhaled a deep breath, and turned to face me. "Natural born dumbass."

"I can't believe you told him to kill me," Riley said.

"He wasn't going to kill anything. Fucking dumbfuck. I hate stupid people," she said.

Riley jumped from her stool and walked toward the front door. After a moment, she returned.

"He's gone," she said.

Stevie shrugged her shoulders. "What? Were you afraid he was going to come back and do something? So he could get that tattoo?"

Riley laughed. "You never know."

Stevie glanced at the clock and shook her head. "I'm frustrated as fuck."

"Why?" Riley asked.

"I need some dick. I've been here for two weeks and haven't been laid yet. I really need somebody to beat my shit up," Stevie said as she turned away.

"You know any bikers with big cocks?" she asked over her shoulder as she sat down at her drawing table.

"Some of the guys from that MC have been in here in the last few weeks, maybe one of 'em will come in sometime," I said as I jumped off my stool.

"A real MC? Like a one-percenter MC?" she asked.

I nodded my head. "Selected Sinners."

"No shit. Fuck yeah, that's what I'm talking about," Stevie said.

"I've got Axton's number. He's the president," Riley said.

Stevie turned around, crossed her arms, and glared at Riley. "You've got the number of the president of a one-percent club on your phone?"

"Uh huh," Riley said as she pulled her phone from her purse.

Stevie glanced in my direction. Behind her on her drawing table, several Styrofoam heads covered in various brightly colored wigs caused me to grin. She had drawn eyes, noses, and lips on each of the otherwise blank faces with the exception of one. The words 'Bad as Fuck" were drawn on the last of the faces, and an arrow pointed toward upward, toward the pink wig.

I shrugged my shoulders. "Friend of the family."

"Tell him I'll trade a nice chest piece for some cock," she said as she turned away.

"No trading sex for tats," I said.

"Fine, tell him I need some dick. I'm sure he'll figure something out," she said as she sat down at her table and began drawing.

"He wants a pic," Riley said.

"You already texted him?" Stevie asked.

Riley nodded her head. "Yeah, he said they're at the bar and he wants a pic."

Stevie slid off the edge of her stool, turned toward us, and tugged against the bottom of her shirt slightly, revealing a reasonable amount of cleavage. After shaking her head back and forth, her purple-tipped hair fell along the top of her chest. She flashed a huge smile and waited.

"Well, quit staring and take a pic, perv," she said.

Riley glanced at me, raised her phone in the air, and snapped a few pictures. Stevie released the bottom of her shirt, turned away, and began drawing.

"All this sex talk…" Riley whispered.

"What's wrong?" I asked innocently.

Riley draped her arms over my shoulders and gazed into my eyes. "I want some biker dick," she whispered.

I glanced around the shop and eventually fixed my eyes on hers. "Anyone in particular?"

She grinned, leaned into me, and kissed me softly. "Tonight, not tomorrow. Not next week. Not when you're caught up. Tonight."

Denying Riley of her much needed dick wasn't on my to-do list. In fact, I had quite the opposite planned.

"Tonight it is," I said with a nod.

"Good," she said. "Now get to hammering that needle in my arm. I'm itching for another tat."

"Like what?" I asked.

"I don't care," she responded. "I'm just wanting something. Maybe add some color?"

"Natural born killer," Stevie hollered over her shoulder.

The unmistakable sound of approaching motorcycles shook the storefront glass. Riley leaned back and turned toward the front of the shop and I jumped from my stool. As I peered over the partition and into the street, bike after bike rode past, turned around, and parked in front

165

of the shop in a row.

Stevie stood on her toes, glanced toward the street, and turned to face Riley. "Tell me that's them."

"It's them," Riley responded.

"A fucking smorgasbord," Stevie said with a laugh.

The door opened and although I didn't see Axton, the first man through the door caused me to take a second glance. It had been roughly twenty years since I'd seen him, but I'd never forget his distinct walk, the smirk he always had on his face, or the prominent scar over his left eye from wrecking the bicycle during the big jump. It just appeared he had grown a few inches and gained sixty pounds or so, all of which seemed to be solid muscle.

I cleared my throat and walked around the partition. "Jackson?"

He shifted his eyes toward me. "Guilty as charged. What can I do..."

I stood and stared. He gazed back at me and eventually his mouth changed from his permanent smirk into a slight smile. "Little man. Holy fucking hell. Little man."

I nodded my head. "How you been?"

"Never better," he said. "That your bagger out front?"

Beaming with pride, I nodded my head. "Yep. Normally park it in the back, but..."

"Finally upgraded from that shitty old Schwinn, huh?" he asked.

"The fucking Schwinn. Shit, wish I still had that fucker. Damn, it's nice to see you," I said. "What the hell are you doing here?"

"Well," he said. "I need a quote for some work, and a couple of the fellas here wanted to meet your other artist, Stevie."

Five men stood behind him, all standing with their arms crossed, and all wearing their leather vests.

I shook my head. "Yeah, my Ol' Lady is friends with Axton, and I think she might have shot him a text about Stevie, but I had…uhhm… no idea you...this is crazy. But…uhhm…yeah…Stevie. She just moved in from San Diego. Hold on…"

I put my arm around Riley and squeezed her shoulder in my hand. "Riley, this is Jackson Shephard. He and I, uhhm…he and I grew up together."

"That we did," he said as he extended his hand. "Pleasure to meet you."

"Pleasure to meet you," Riley said as she shook his hand.

"And this…" I paused and turned around.

Stevie stood immediately to my right and a few feet behind me.

"This is Stevie," I said as I waved my hand in her direction.

He nodded his head. "Well, I'm not here for that. I got an Ol' Lady."

"Listen up," Stevie hollered, interrupting our conversation and clearly taking charge of the situation.

"I don't ever fuck with anyone but bikers, and I'll only fuck with a biker if he's got a big dick. I've got a foul mouth, a shitty attitude, and an insatiable desire. I'm no whore, and I won't be treated like one. If you're looking to hit it and quit it, you can forget it. I'm not your girl. If you want an Ol' Lady who'll out drink ya, out fuck ya, and probably out cuss ya, I'm your girl," she shouted.

"How many's that leave?" she asked.

Jackson chuckled and turned around. "Vince?"

A tall muscular guy with dark hair and an obvious attitude sauntered toward Jackson. Stevie stepped to the side, studied him, and crossed her arms in front of her chest.

"What's your road name?" she asked.

He pointed to his patch, "Vince."

Stevie coughed a laugh. "That's your *road name*?"

"Yep. Name's Stephen. They call me Vince," he said.

"You qualified?" she asked.

He stood and stared for a moment and then shook his head and grinned. "Look, I came up here after Slice showed us your pic at the bar. Thought you were a cute little fucker. Seem a little crazy for my taste now that I'm here. I ain't lookin' to add a bunch of drama in my fucking life. Shit, I just got rid of an Ol' Lady for bein' a drama queen. Well, that and a whore. Nice to meet ya, though."

Jackson chuckled and shook his head. The thought of it all seemed crazy to me. Riley stood at my side shifting her eyes between Stevie and Vince, anxiously waiting for someone to speak. As I suspected, Stevie broke the silence.

"I'm not a whore, and I'm not crazy. I'm just some chick that loves bikes, appreciates the freedom of riding, and appreciates one-percenters for being who they are. I'm a lot of fucking fun, really," she said.

He shrugged his shoulders. "What's a one percenter mean to you? Who am I?"

I glanced at Riley and grinned. This was good shit for sure.

"Well, being an outlaw. Fuck the man, fuck society. Riding isn't a fucking hobby, and it's not really *a way of life*, it *is* life. You see that mountain bike outside?" she asked.

"Chained up by the door?" he asked.

Stevie nodded her head. "I rode that motherfucker six miles here instead of taking a ride in a cage."

"Is that so," he said.

Stevie nodded her head. "So…"

168

"I'll be back," he said with a nod. "We'll go for a ride."

As he turned and walked out the door, everyone followed but Jackson.

"Crazy fuckers," Jackson said.

"So what were you wanting done?" I asked.

"Wanted a quote for a pin-up girl on my forearm," he said.

"You busy Tuesday? Say noon?" I asked.

He shook his head. "Guess not."

"It's on me," I said. "For old times."

"Appreciate ya," he said.

"Well, that was a fucking bust," Stevie said.

I nodded my head in acknowledgement. "Maybe try a softer side next time."

"That was my soft side," she said.

"Alright. I'm gonna get back to it," Jackson said as he held out his hand.

"Nice seeing ya," I said as I shook his hand.

"Riley, Stevie, nice meeting ya," he said.

"Same here," Riley said.

"Bring Vince back with ya," Stevie shouted.

As he walked away, Jackson waved his hand in the air.

Stevie turned to face Riley, sighed and shook her head. "Want a hot investment tip?"

"Sure," Riley responded.

"Buy some Duracell stock," Stevie said flatly.

Although Riley didn't appear to catch the joke, I laughed to myself, knowing if I had anything to say about it, Riley wouldn't need batteries for a long, long time.

RILEY

Being in a relationship with a man who preferred to control my every action left little room for me to make decisions sexually; or otherwise for that matter. The last eight months had left me feeling sexually frustrated, and although I had looked so forward to the relief once the day came, I was somewhat apprehensive about everything.

I wouldn't trade Blake or what we had together for anything, and I truly believed we stumbled into each other by design, but thinking I was the more promiscuous one of the couple left me feeling awkward and not much like a girl.

I wanted him to take charge, but I realized having him do so was all but impossible for so many reasons. So, I swallowed my pride, set aside my selfish thoughts, and decided to take the reins for at least a little while.

"Okay, if anything happens that freaks you out or creeps you out, just say so and we'll stop," I said.

He nodded his head and laughed lightly. "I'll be fine."

"You say that, but…"

"I'll be fine."

"Okay," I said. "This isn't a contest, and you won't be graded. I'll tell you what I like or if something's weird, and you do the same, okay?"

"Okay."

"Uhhm. Get undressed," I said as I waved my hand in his direction.
"Everything?" he asked.

I grinned at the thought of seeing him naked. "Yeah, toss it."

He nodded his head. It seemed almost like some weird dream, thinking we hadn't seen each other naked and we'd been seeing each other for almost six weeks. The time had come, however, and I was more than ready. As I watched him fumbling with his belt, I pulled off my shirt, bra, and started to take off my shorts.

As I pushed my shorts past my hips, I glanced in his direction. With his jeans now around his ankles and his boxers slightly above them, his cock stood at full attention. It appeared Blake was as ready as I was for whatever we decided to do. I stood for a moment and stared at him.

As he stood there holding his shirt in his hand, covered in tattoos with his biceps bulging, his broad chest heaving from his breathing, and his washboard stomach tapering to the little "V" thing he had going on at his waist, I decided quickly it was time to move forward.

"Okay," I said as I shoved my shorts down my legs hurriedly. "First things first."

"Okay," he said.

He had shared with me since our discussion at Waterfront that his sexual experiences consisted of masturbation, watching videos, and enjoying the one time I had sucked his cock. Sexually speaking, that had been it for him. He had zero experience, and in addition, he was a little apprehensive considering his past.

I pointed to my bed.

I pointed to the bed and wagged my finger. "Lay on your back."

He tossed his shirt on the pile of clothes at his feet. His tattooed chest, well-defined abs, and slim waist were enough to have my mouth watering and my pussy dripping.

"Okay, so you've seen videos. Have you ever seen one of a guy licking pussy?" I asked.

He nodded his head. "Yeah, a bunch of times."

"Okay, well. That's the first step. Sex always starts with a good pussy licking. Always," I said.

I viewed his lack of experience as a chance for me to begin our sexual relationship with the processes and procedures in place that should be a prerequisite to sex anyway.

"Okay," he said.

I raised my index finger in the air and tried to keep from grinning. "Kissing, oral sex, and then penetration. And always in that order."

He nodded his head and positioned himself on the bed on his back. With his cock sticking straight up in the air it was almost as if he was begging me to use him. As much as I wanted to just climb on top of him and reverse cowgirl him into a fucking coma, I did my best to follow my own rules.

I sat down on the edge of the bed, reached for his cock, and stroked it in my hand.

"This is just bullshit foreplay, it's allowed," I giggled as I leaned forward and kissed him.

I was beyond ready. As much as I enjoyed kissing Blake, as far as I was concerned, I had six weeks experience at doing so, and six weeks of sexual torture from not having sex. I kissed him for three or four minutes, which in my mind was three or four minutes too damned long.

"Stay right where you are. I'm going to climb on top of you and push my butt in your face. It might seem weird, but it'll work out pretty good, really. Just finger me and lick my pussy. I'll tell you if you're doing it right," I said.

He nodded his head.

This is ridiculous.

I straddled him, inched my way backward, and raised my ass in the air slightly. As I stared down at his twitching cock, he wasted no time getting started.

Holy shit.

I grabbed his cock in my hand, stroked it a couple times, and wrapped my lips around it. As he sucked and licked my pussy like he had some kind of formal training, I bucked my hips back and forth, fucking his mouth like he'd paid me to do so.

His tongue flicked across my swollen nub with precision while his finger worked in and out of my wetness. In return of the favor, I sucked his dick hesitantly and attempted to shift my focus to him licking my pussy.

As much as I enjoyed sucking his dick, the selfish side of me realized if I continued, and succeeded at making him reach climax, the sex would be over for a while. For the sake of my sanity, and to assure I reached climax from his oral procedures beforehand, I decided to suck his cock as slowly as I was able.

This process worked and worked well until...

Holy shit he can lick a pussy...

"Oh fuck. Keep doing that. Right there," I howled.

I held still while he nibbled on my clit and finger fucked me into a slight state of paralysis.

I arched my back and pushed my pussy against his mouth while he tongue fucked me into an orgasm; not because I wanted to, but because I could do nothing else. I was frozen in time, space, and sexual bliss. As

174

he continued to educate himself on the art of oral pleasure, I squealed out loud and covered his face in my wet juices.

I did my very best to hold still and wallow in the feeling for as long as I could.

"Don't move," I whispered. "You made me cum."

"Okay, he said.

"You ever heard of reverse cowgirl?" I asked as I slid my pussy along his ripped mid-section.

I sat up on his hips, staring down at his thick cock. There was no need for any further explanation. People had been fucking long before there was a means of communicating verbally, and doing so without any problems that I'd ever heard of. I needed to feel his fat cock inside of me and I didn't feel a need to explain how, why, or where.

I glanced over my shoulder, grinned, and reached toward his cock. After gripping it firmly in my hand, I lifted my ass slightly and guided it into my swollen wet pussy as I lowered myself onto the tip.

As I felt it begin to penetrate me, I pressed my hands onto his thighs and arched my back.

"Watch. It helps, really," I said over my shoulder.

I had no idea if he heard me or not. I was all too eager to get started. Without warning, preparation, or any idea of how well his thick oversized shaft was going to fit inside of me, I began to work my hips like a stripper on a pole.

His cock felt like it was in my chest. I exhaled a loud moan out into the room, took a deep breath, and began my journey to achieve another much needed orgasm at Blake's expense.

As I squeezed his thighs in my hands and bucked my hips back and forth, his thick shaft worked in and out of my tight wet pussy no differently than if it had been fashioned solely for my delight.

A matter of a few seconds and no more than three or four strokes into the affair, his cock begin to swell. It was all I needed. I relaxed, slowed my pace, and attempted to milk him of his juices. As I felt him begin to erupt inside of me, I gripped his legs in my hand, bit my lip, and arched my back.

"Oh my God," he growled as his cock swelled to twice its size.

And he exploded.

"Holy…"

"Fuck…" I bellowed.

The orgasm felt as if it came from my deep within my pussy, which was something I wasn't used to. Orgasms in my past were more of a sensation of my skin and outer region, but this felt as if it developed inside my soul.

From my nipples to the tip of his deeply situated cock, my body tingled. I blinked my eyes repeatedly, fully expecting something to change, but it didn't. Satisfied I had truly found my mate, and Blake had found his calling in life, I lifted my throbbing pussy from his slowly diminishing rod and collapsed onto his legs, chest down.

"That was incredible," I said, my face resting on his thigh.

He raised himself up on his elbows slightly. "It was awesome."

I tilted my head to the side, turned to face him, and grinned. Looking at him from my vantage point allowed me to glance all the way up his torso, seeing his each and every well-defined muscle. At the top of his mid-section, his swollen chest heaved up and down.

I glanced to the side at his tattooed arms. The tattoos on his sweat-covered biceps glistened as he situated his arms. He gazed down at me and grinned.

"How uhhm. How long until we can do it again?" he asked.

"What do you mean?"

"Until we can fuck again?" he asked as he ran his fingers through his hair.

I made a feeble attempt to shrug my shoulders. "Uhhm, whenever you can get it up."

"Okay. Give me a few minutes," he said.

My eyes widened considerably. "You're not done?"

He chuckled and shook his head as he ran his fingers through his hair again. "Done? No, I'm not done. But I may have some bad news."

"Uhhm, huh? Bad news?"

He grinned and nodded his head. "The next time I visit Doc Racine, I'm going to have to tell him I'm a sex addict, and this time I won't be lying."

I grinned in return.

Thank God.

BLAKE

My subconscious fears had become reality. Sex wasn't something I desired or wanted from time to time, it was an addiction. At first I believed it to be no different than anything else new to me. As a child and as an adult, whatever was new to me - as long as I enjoyed it - received all undivided attention. As a kid, my new bicycle was my focus. As an adult, my newest motorcycle received my attention. Whenever I made a new tattoo machine or purchased a new television, they were the objects of my desire until something newer or more interesting came along.

I dismissed my initial desire to have repeated sex with Riley to this old pattern of behavior for the first few days, but now, after two weeks of time had passed, I realized I had a problem.

Choosing whether or not to address the problem was something I had yet to decide.

The chairs used by tattoo artists are chosen as a matter of personal preference, and typically most artists choose to recondition or rebuild a vintage dentist's chair. My personal favorite was the Ritter from the 1930's I had recovered and refinished to an almost new state. One advantage of using the Dentist chair was the chair's ability to adjust into almost any position from flat to upright, and everything in between.

At present, my chair was almost flat, with the upper portion slightly elevated. Riley was in it backward, with her legs dangling over the portion designed for the head, and her pussy elevated to a perfect height.

And I stood behind the chair doing what Riley described as the required precursor to sex, her moaning echoed throughout the shop.

"If you keep wiggling around, I'm going to spin this chair around and shove you full of dick," I said as I pulled my face from between her legs.

"No. No. Don't do that. I'll hold still, I swear," she begged.

"You better," I said as I pressed my palms against her inner thighs.

She lowered her head onto the cushion of the chair. "I will."

After watching her sink her upper teeth into her lower lip, I buried my face between her legs and began to suck on her clit.

As I fingered her slowly and methodically, I flicked my tongue against her nub. Appearing to be uncertain if she wanted to continue or run away, she raised her hips for a few seconds, allowed me to have my way with her, and eventually lowered her hips and began to squirm along the leather cushion in an attempt to get away.

Five minutes into her indecisive behavior, and I did my best to appear to be angry with her.

"That's it," I bellowed as I slapped my hand against the side of the chair, causing it to spin in a circle.

"What?" she snapped back as she spun past me.

"You can't fucking hold still. That's *it*," I said.

"I've had so many orgasms I feel like I'm going to pop or something, I'm sorry, it's sensitive," she said as the chair came to a stop.

Without warning, I pressed the lever on the side of the chair, lowering the end of it to a flat position; causing her hips to be at the same elevation as her head. Now with her knees bent and her legs dangling over the end of the chair, I reached for my belt as I shook my head from side-to-side.

She batted her eyes and grinned. "What?"

"Here's what," I said as I pushed my jeans to my thighs.

I grabbed her ankles, pulled her toward me slightly, and guided myself into her wet pussy.

"Oh God…" she moaned as I slowly pushed myself into her.

I watched the length of my cock slowly disappear. After burying it as deep as possible, I pulled back slightly, grinning at the sight of the glistening shaft as it slowly slid free of her dripping pussy. Seeing her excitement spread all over my throbbing flesh was enough to feed me with energy for an entire evening.

"You know what I like about fucking you in the shop?" I asked as I began to work my hips back and forth.

"Uhhm…what?" she asked, her breathing already becoming labored.

I exhaled my response with another quick thrust of my cock. "Everything."

"You're…breaking…" she paused and raised herself onto her elbows. "The rules…No fucking in…the shop."

"Rules are made to be broken," I said as I continued to work my hips back and forth, attempting to maintain focus on my cock as it repeatedly disappeared inside of her.

I found the process of having sex to be much more than entertaining; it was an almost magical experience. The human body was designed to do exactly what we were doing, and I planned on continuing until I was incapable.

Riley sat up slightly in the chair and shifted her eyes to my crotch as I continued to pound away.

"Watch, it helps," I said sarcastically, repeating her comment from the first night we had sex.

"I can't watch…for…long," she said.

I grinned, gripped her waist in my hands, and pulled my hips back slowly. As my stiff dick slid from her wet folds, she sighed. After a moment of staring down at the head of my cock, I shifted my eyes slowly along her body, eventually stopping at her face.

The most beautiful woman in the world is made even more so by simply shoving her full of a good stiff dick.

"Ready?" I asked.

"For?"

"Ready?"

"Yep," she said with a nod.

I watched my cock disappear until my balls were against her ass crack. After a few seconds of savoring the feeling of her warmth, I began to pound away without mercy. My physical condition wasn't the best in the world, but my determination was unmatched by any man.

As I thrust my hips back and forth, taking as long of strokes as I was able to without completely pulling out, Riley's labored breathing became apparent and louder than the sound of our slapping flesh or the music playing in the background.

After a few minutes, she began to wail.

The sound of her reaching climax was all I needed.

My call to action.

As she cried out into the room, her pussy contracted around my throbbing flesh. I buried myself deep inside of her and groaned as I exploded every ounce of my love deep within her soul.

"That…"

"Was…"

"Amazing," she said.

"I love fucking you," I said.

She exhaled a heavy sigh. "Good, because I love it when you fuck me."

I leaned forward, kissed her stomach, and stood for a moment absorbing her beauty. As her eyes fell closed, I grinned and shuffled to the bathroom. After cleaning myself in the sink, I pulled up my jeans, buckled my belt, and gazed into the mirror.

My life had changed drastically. I had been living in a world complicated with a combination of fact and fiction and remained somewhere in between in a sea of uncertainty. Often incapable of separating what was genuine from what was contrived; my mind resided in limbo. Now, attempting to comprehend the reality of the dream I was living in seemed all too confusing.

It was almost as if none of it could be real.

The bathroom door opened. I stared blankly at Riley's reflection in the mirror. I reached out and pressed my hand against the cold glass, obstructing the image of her face. After a moment, I slid my hand to the side and blocked my own reflection.

As her hand touched the bare skin of my upper arm, I turned and glanced over my shoulder.

I needed proof.

"I want you to do something for me," I said.

She squeezed my arm lightly. "Name it."

"I want you to tattoo me," I said.

"What?" she gasped.

"Just something simple, I'll guide you through it," I said as I shifted my eyes toward the mirror.

As I gazed at our reflection, she leaned forward and rested her chin on my shoulder.

     "If that's what you want," she said.

     "It is," I responded.

     I simply needed to know for sure.

RILEY

Before I was ever in a relationship, I had a vision of what I wanted the man in my life to be. It was more of a dream, but consisted of an outline of the qualities he would possess nonetheless. Blake was not only everything I had once dreamed of, but much more.

Blake was unpredictable in so many respects, yet so much of what he did was foreseeable and expected. It was almost as if he had moments or waves of uncertainty which required him stepping out of himself to take a look at everything around him from the outside.

During these times, I found him to be interesting, artistic, and genuine. It wasn't that I questioned his sincerity or authenticity in his normal manner of living, but when he was uncertain of his surroundings there was much more depth to his being.

"Just a line across your wrist?" I asked.

He glanced up, grinned, and nodded his head once. "That's it."

Although he had instructed me on how to do it, I sat with the machine in my shaking hand uncertain if I could actually proceed.

"What if I go too deep? Or not deep enough?" I asked.

"I'll tell you. Just do your best to follow the stencil. Now dip it in the ink and go," he said.

I fixed my eyes on his face. He stared intently at the line he had drawn across his wrist and waited. I dipped the needle in the well, stepped on the switch, and lifted the machine to his wrist. As I pressed the tip of the needle into his skin, the sound changed from a loose rattle to a dull drone.

"Perfect," he sighed.

"Go a little slower," he said.

I followed the line with the tip of the needle. The ink pooled behind the machine and ran along his wrist and onto the leather support. After a few seconds, I was done.

I lifted my foot from the pedal, stopping the machine. After setting it aside, I reached for the soap, sprayed it into a paper towel and wiped the area clean.

I did it.

A three inch wide line across his wrist, heavy at one end and a little lighter on the other was now permanently etched into his skin.

I felt powerful; as if somehow simply doing the tattoo had made me part of who Blake was, or maybe that it had bound us together even more than we already were.

As simple as the process was, the feeling was indescribable. I quickly came to understand why Blake enjoyed tattooing as much as he did. There was a part of him in each and every person he tattooed, and a small part of them remained with him when they left.

"It's kind of blurry on that one end," I said as I studied his wrist.

"It's perfect," he said.

"Blurry," I repeated as I shook my head.

He gazed down at the tattoo and flexed his forearm. "It's perfect. Blurred lines; it's when fact and fiction become indiscernible. Fantasy and reality fade into a color of grey yarn and you become tangled up in it and can't escape into the world of black and white you desperately need as proof of the reality of life itself."

He shifted his eyes upward and smiled, "I fucking love it."

"I like it more now," I said.

"Riley," he said as turned toward me.

"I love you," he said as his eyes met mine.

I gazed into his eyes. Glistening of browns and greens, they peered back at me as proof of his sincerity.

I didn't disagree, but I wasn't prepared to hear it. As my eyes welled with tears and I felt my throat tighten, I reached for his hand. And, as I lightly squeezed his fingers in my palm, I somehow swallowed the lump in my throat and spoke.

"And I, Blake West, love you."

BLAKE

The pieces of my life I had always found distasteful were never able to be cast aside, forgotten, or simply walked away from. They remained a part of me, and often became part of my day-to-day decision making, reminding me further of their significance in my life.

They lingered in my mind, loitering about in my life because they were unresolved, and resolution was something I found to be impossible or unattainable. I believed my mind had the capacity to be cleansed of all problems my past created if I was simply able to confront the doer of evil.

The human mind strives to fix what it believes to be broken. Consequently, if I believed something to be in need of repair, I felt I could find no peace until I exhausted myself in the process of doing so.

I watched the pen form the words on the paper. I felt writing to be more intimate than typing a letter and printing it. After much thought, extended moments of pause, and a few tears, I stared down at the completed work.

You may or may not have noticed, but I did not begin this letter with any kind of a greeting or recognize you at all by any type of introduction. Additionally, you will find the envelope to be addressed to your inmate number, and not your name. It was not an oversight, but something I truly felt was necessary.

To me, you are a monster, and clearly the opposite of what I believe to be human. I live in a world of grey because of you although I certainly realize a black and white one surrounds me.

To recognize darkness as being so, we must have an understanding of what is light. To truly comprehend goodness, an understanding of what we believe to be evil is necessary.

You define evil.

I know this because I am as good as I am able to be. I believe I am not as wholesome or proper as I may have been had you not taken my parents from me, but as good as is possible considering the circumstances of my life. I refuse, however, to credit you with creating what little evil resides within me, and I take all responsibility for what little I possess. I reserve hope of one day obtaining a personal sense of perfection, as I am still young and have a lifetime to make whatever corrections I feel I must to do so.

You took something from me which can never be replaced or corrected. I am writing this letter not for you, but for me. I believe conveying my feelings will provide me with a sense of closure and a small bit of satisfaction in knowing although it wasn't done in a physical sense, I confronted you.

If there is a heaven, and I suspect there is, I find comfort in knowing when I leave this earth I will not have the potential of stumbling upon you or the wake of evil that follows in your footprints.

Until the day you burn in hell I will look down upon you as what you are.

With what little forgiveness I am able to offer.

Blake West

I folded the paper neatly, inserted it into the envelope, and sealed the letter. If nothing else, writing it provided me with a sense of relief so profound, I found it unnerving I hadn't done it sooner.

Riley's confrontation of me the day at the lake, our revelation of secrets, and my admittance of what happened to my parents was the first time I had spoken to anyone about my loss short of Doc Racine. Admitting what happened made the loss become real, and the reality of it all caused me to deal with it.

I may have been a few decades late in resolving matters, but found satisfaction in doing so nonetheless.

I picked up my phone and typed a text message.

Write your letter yet?

I pressed send, tossed my phone on the counter, and stood from my seat.

Riley was good for me in so many ways. Our having found each other wasn't by design or the result of an exhaustive search on either of our parts. We were two people who were looking for nothing yet found everything; and we found it in each other.

Knowing the odds of us finding each other was more than merely happenstance, yet further understanding what caused us to meet was beyond my comprehension, I was only able to sit back and thank God for gracing me with her presence.

My phone beeped. I swiped my finger across the screen and pressed the message with the tip of my thumb.

Yes. Pick me up?

I fumbled with the keys, pressed send, and stared at the screen.

Be there in ten

A smiley face came back immediately. I glanced down at it and grinned.

BLURRED LINES

Riley had her own reasons to be angry with the world, society, and the system, but she remained peaceful inside and out. One day I hoped to be a little more like her, but until that day came, I would have to remain satisfied that I was good enough to be by her side.

And by her side I intended to remain.

RILEY

I sat on the porch and clutched the envelope in my hand. Writing the letter provided me with tremendous satisfaction, and I hoped mailing it would provide even more. Either way, it was a step I felt needed to be taken, and taking it wasn't necessarily easy.

Knowing the man who killed Blake's parents and my father was still alive, and in a few short days would be holding the very paper which I wrote my feelings upon was creepy and satisfying at the same time. As I tapped the edge of the envelope on my knee and waited, I grinned at the thought of the simple but effective words I had written.

Mr. Mastick,

You took my mother's husband, my father, and my boyfriend's parents, but I refuse to allow you to take even a shred of me.

In fact, I'm giving you something.

I read you were a germaphobe and were even allowed to wear gloves in the courtroom. Well, after a reasonable amount of research and a few telephone calls to the department of corrections, I have confirmed you are now imprisoned and without gloves.

So, I find tremendous comfort in providing you with this information: I pissed all over this paper.

Fuck off and die.

Riley Campbell, a true survivor

As soon as I recognized the sound of Blake's motorcycle coming up the block I stood, grabbed my helmet, and ran to the street. Riding on the motorcycle was now one of my favorite things to do. Stevie was right, it was a feeling of freedom I couldn't find doing anything else.

It made perfect sense why so many veterans of war, police officers, and former prisoners rode motorcycles. The ride provided a sense of freedom nothing else could provide. The feeling of being on the bike and flying down the road cleared my mind, and I was sure it cleared the minds of many others like me.

I shoved the letter in my pocket, pulled the helmet onto my head, pulled the strap tight, and climbed onto the seat as soon as he came to a stop at the curb.

"Ready," I said as I tapped him on the side.

Without speaking, he released the clutch and slowly picked up speed. As we rode through the neighborhood, I leaned to the side and gazed out at the road ahead of us.

"Beautiful day," I shouted.

"Gorgeous," he said.

I leaned back in the seat and pressed myself against the backrest. There was really no need for me to hold onto him as he rode, the support behind me provided plenty of stability, but I did it because I liked to. Touching him allowed me to continuously believe that he, and all of what we shared together, was real.

We turned into the parking lot across from the grocery store and parked beside the big blue mailbox. I got off the bike, unstrapped my helmet, and pulled the letter from my pocket.

"I've got a stamp if you need one," I said.

"Got it covered," he said as he stepped off the bike.

I pulled the door to the big steel box open and dropped my letter in the tray. He stepped beside me, dropped his letter on top, and turned to face me.

"Well," he said.

"Any departing words or anything before I close it?" I asked.

He shook his head.

"I pissed on it," I said.

"Pissed on what?"

"Pissed on my letter. He's a germaphobe. So, I pissed on it and told him so in the letter. It's the least I could do," I said, still standing there holding the door open.

He reached for the opening, pulled out his letter, and tossed it onto the asphalt beside his motorcycle.

"What are you doing?" I asked.

He glanced over each shoulder, unzipped his pants, and started whistling.

"Does that really work?" I asked.

After a few seconds, a stream of urine splashed against the envelope. As the puddle got so large it began to run toward the sidewalk, he stopped, shook his cock dry, and zipped up his pants.

"Hold on a minute," he said as he opened the saddlebag on the side of the motorcycle.

After removing a pair of pliers from the toolkit, he picked up the letter and grinned.

"Look out," he said as he dropped it into the mailbox tray.

I nodded my head smiled until it hurt. "Good idea, huh?"

"Great," he said. "Close that thing and lets go get some ice cream."

Mailing pissed covered letters to murderers and getting ice cream with a tattooed biker who had developed a kink for spanking my ass while fucking me.

Sundays had always been the most boring day of the week for me. And then I met Blake West.

BLAKE

After adding Stevie as an employee, business had steadily picked up a little each day. Now we were as busy as I had always expected I would one day become, and the steady flow of clients was a nice departure from what I had become accustomed to.

"Uhhm, Jackson's next, and you're thirty minutes behind," Riley said as I came out of the bathroom.

"I'll get caught up, don't worry. Send him back," I said as I turned toward my work station.

"Have a seat. How's that pin-up tat looking?" I asked as Jackson walked up beside me.

"Damned thing's almost healed. You've got the lightest hands I've ever seen. Better than getting them in the joint, that's for sure," he said as he rotated his forearm.

I gazed down at the piece I had tattooed on his arm two weeks prior; an old school pin-up girl holding a steaming pie. According to him, it was a reminder of the love of his life, an avid cook and former restaurateur. It looked amazing. No swelling, vivid color, and each line was clean and crisp.

"So, how's the Ol' Lady like it?" I asked as he sat down in the chair.

"Loves it," he responded.

"Good. And today we're doing the devil piece, right?" I asked.

197

"You got it," he said.

I picked up the drawing I had prepared and held it up for him to see.

"Fuck yeah. Looks good," he said.

"Look a lot better shaded and with a little color. Only color you want is in the devil's head, right?" I asked.

"I was thinking it'd stand out better that way, but I'm open for your suggestions," he responded.

"I think it'll look good just the way you want it," I said as I pulled on a new pair of gloves.

I wiped down his bicep, shaved the area, and pressed the stencil onto his arm. After peeling it from his skin, I gazed down at the piece. The phrase *The Devil Looks After His Own* with devil's head in place of the word "devil".

After pulling a new machine from the drawer and installing a new needle, I poured black, white and red ink into three ink wells. After dipping the needle in the black ink, I turned toward Jackson.

"Say the word," I said.

"There aren't too many things in life I look forward too, little man. Getting some new ink is one of 'em. Get to it," he said.

There wasn't anything much more unnerving than a young girl who wanted a tattoo to look cool or fit in, and although she made the appointment and payed for the service, she had in no way mentally committed to the idea of it all. Half way through the session, she would inevitably be squirming all around in the chair and whining about the pain, continuously asking when I was going to be finished. Having someone like Jackson sit and allow me to perform my work without question, complaint, or further suggestion was priceless.

I pressed the heel of my palm against the surface of his skin and watched as the needle followed the line of the devil's head. After a few minutes, the outline of head was complete.

"Everything good?" I asked as I dipped the needle again.

"The only part I don't like is when you stop," he said.

I nodded my head once. "That's what I like to hear."

I traced the outline of each individual letter and then filled the letters with ink. The script Jackson had chosen, Almendra, was much different than the font Axton had used on his arm. I felt the script complimented the tattoo perfectly. The tattooing process with the script took roughly forty-five minutes.

"Still good?" I asked as soon as I was done with the script.

"Still Good," he responded.

One thing about being a tattoo artist I had always found interesting was that if I didn't take time to speak to my client, they seemed to feel talking wasn't allowed during a tattoo. On the other hand, if I chose to speak to a client, all of a sudden I became their therapist, and was forced to listen to any and everything that happened to them from childhood to sitting in the chair.

Talking to Jackson was something I actually wanted to do. I had looked up to him while we were living together, and he was really the closest thing to a brother I had. Although he was six or eight years my senior, I lived with him for roughly five years, and at the time, we developed a bond similar to what two brothers would have developed.

It seemed the portions of my childhood I preferred to forget lingered, and the events I had expectation of retaining vivid memories of faded into faint recollections. The opposite of what I wished was true, but something I was forced to accept. One thing I did remember was the day Jackson left, I cried.

"You ever wonder what happened to Sharkey and that family?" I asked as I shaded the horns of the devil's head.

"Found out they moved to Oklahoma," he said.

I released the pedal and lifted the needle from his skin. My hands began to shake. The one thing that prevented me from acting on my urge to seek revenge for what he and his son had done to me was that I didn't know where they had moved to.

After leaving the foster home, I wandered around the city, seeking a place to call home, but never living in anything more than a shitty apartment. Initially I perceived what had happened as simply a part of being an orphan, and not having siblings or parents. A price I had to pay, I supposed, for being different and not having a family to love me.

As I grew older, I grew angrier. My initial hope was to become a police officer and make a difference in the lives of all I was able. After the academy, a short stint as a patrol officer ended when I determined not all civilians are created equal in the eyes of the police.

Something I had always suspected was true. The color of a man's skin, or the location of his residence made a huge difference in how calls were dispatched, who was arrested, and what charges were filed.

When I finally decided I needed to confront the preacher and his son, I found that they had moved, and although I tried to find them, found nothing. I soon gave up, deciding there was no real value in digging up the bones of my past.

Considering how mailing the letter caused me to feel, I now realized confronting them in any manner would be therapeutic for me.

"You alright?" he asked.

"Uhhm, yeah. I'm good. Hold on a minute," I said as I pulled off my gloves.

"I uhhm. I need a quick break. A cigarette," I said.

He nodded his head and looked down at his arm. "If I join you, this'll be alright, wont it?"

"Sure, let me cover it real quick," I said as I turned toward my box.

I stretched a piece of cellophane wrap over his arm and secured it to itself. After grabbing my cigarettes and rolling them into my sleeve, I shouted toward Riley, who was seated at the partition talking to a client.

"Going out for a smoke," I shouted.

"Okay," she said over her shoulder.

Jackson followed me outside, and stood quietly while I smoked the first half of the cigarette. As I leaned against the wall and wondered if I truly needed to know where Sharkey lived, he cleared his throat and spoke.

"You asked about the old man at the foster home. When I answered, I noticed you started shaking. You alright?" he asked.

I shrugged my shoulders. "You know where he is for sure?"

He nodded his head. "Found out during my court case. They had to find him for a presentence investigation. I have his address, why?"

"Might need to pay him a visit," I said as I lifted the cigarette to my mouth.

"Guessing by how that hand's still shaking you aren't looking to shake the man's hand. You want to talk about it?" he asked.

I shrugged again, took a long drag from the cigarette, and glanced at glowing end as I inhaled the smoke.

He was the closest thing to a brother I ever had. I felt I could talk to him, and even if I didn't tell him everything, telling him something may allow him to give more sound advice. And, as far as I knew, he may have been abused as well.

I exhaled the smoke, tossed the butt in the alley, and lit another cigarette. After taking another long puff, I gazed blankly at my motorcycle and exhaled the smoke.

"Him and his son took me when I was eight and molested me. They did it more than once. I'm thinking I may want revenge or something, I don't know," I said.

He stared beyond my motorcycle and out into the alley. "Son-of-a-bitch. They never fucked with me, but I always wondered."

I turned to face him. I don't know if I felt he should provide answers, an offer to help, an apology for not providing me protection as a child, or just a willing ear, but I stood and gazed at him feeling as if I wanted something.

I just didn't know what.

But Jackson seemed to.

"Cocksucker," he said as he crossed his arms in front of his chest. "Don't know what you got planned or what you're going to plan, but I'm afraid I'm going to have to be involved in this."

My mouth curled into a slight grin. "You think so?"

He shook his head from side-to-side, inhaled a deep breath, and gazed down at his boots.

"People that fuck with kids never stop. Never. I can't really live knowing he did something to you and not go take care of it. Hell, it might even be better if you just stay here. I'll take a couple of the fellas with me and we'll take care of him," he said.

I shrugged my shoulders and glared. "Why the hell would they want to go? They don't know me?"

He turned his head to the side and widened his eyes. "Because they're my brothers. And there isn't one of them that wouldn't volunteer to go take care of that piece of shit. Hell, they'll be in a fucking fight to see who gets to go."

"I need to do this," I said. "I been fighting with this my whole life."

"If it's all the same to you, I'd rather not have you doing it alone," he said.

I nodded my head. "Okay by me."

He extended his hand.

As I shook his hand in mine, he pulled me into him and hugged me. Although it seemed strange at first, it was comforting. As he patted his hand against my back, I did the same. He released me from his arms and pointed down at my bike.

"Gets cold outside, how do you get to work?" he asked.

I nodded my head toward the motorcycle. "It's all I got."

"Interesting," he said.

He turned and pulled the door open to the shop and held it.

"After you," I said as I motioned toward the door.

"You go first, little man. I've got your back," he said with a laugh.

And, although he laughed, I knew he wasn't joking.

RILEY

I felt slightly guilty having my mother to consult with for any and every problem, concern, idea, or situation I got myself into, knowing Blake had no one but me. I hoped since he and his old friend Jackson were reunited, he could possibly talk to him about his concerns and ideas concerning life.

"When you met dad, had you already had a boyfriend, or was he your first?" I asked.

"Why would you ask such a thing?" she said.

I shrugged my shoulders and pulled a container of pasta salad out of the refrigerator. "How old's the pasta?"

"I made it yesterday," she responded.

"Okay," I said.

I grabbed two bowls, two forks, and walked to the table. "Just wondering, I guess," I said as I pulled the chair from the table.

"I had a boyfriend before your father," she said as I sat down.

I carefully flipped some of the pasta salad out of the container and into a bowl. "Did you think you were in love with the other guy?"

"I suppose so," she responded.

I slid the bowl across the table. "Here."

"And when you met dad, then what did you think? About the first guy?" I asked.

She poked her fork into the bowl of pasta salad, raised it to her mouth, and paused. "What's this about?"

I scooped the remaining pasta salad into my bowl.

"I used to think I loved Stephen. And now that I've met Blake, I'm mad that I ever thought I loved him. I know I didn't," I said.

"It's pretty common. Probably more so than you'd think," she said.

"I want to take it back. Like go tell him 'hey, asshole, I never loved you. I was mistaken, sorry' or something. It makes me mad," I said.

She chuckled and poked the fork of pasta into her mouth. "There's very few people who find their true love the first time. But when we do find that person, I think we finally realize what love is. Your father was mine."

"Blake's mine," I said.

She nodded her head and smiled. "I like him. He calls me ma'am. It's cute."

I wagged my fork in her direction. "And he bought me a helmet. Don't forget that."

"I won't," she said.

"I want to make a proposal," she said.

"Huh?"

She drug the fork past her pursed lips and stared down at the tines. "A proposal. Or whatever you want to call it. I want something from you two, and I'm getting older by the minute, so don't think about it too long."

"What are you talking about?" I asked.

"I want to start a tradition. I want you two to come here on Sunday nights and have dinner," she said. "I've always wanted that."

I shrugged my shoulders. "Is that it?"

She nodded her head as she stared down into her bowl. "Did you put all the shrimp in your half?"

"No," I said as I poked a piece of pasta, and then a piece of shrimp.

She raised her eyebrows and glared at me. "Hmm."

"So," she said. "What do you think about my request."

"I like it," I said. "I'll ask him."

"I thought maybe you could cook one week, maybe me the next, or we could do it together," she said.

"Blake likes to grill," I said.

"I think that's a man thing. Your father grilled the best chicken I've ever eaten," she said.

"Well, I'll talk to him and see what he thinks. I bet he'll say okay. I can't imagine what it's like for him to have no family," I said as I poked another piece of shrimp.

"I wonder if he ever had kids in the foster home who stole food from him" she said as she reached for my bowl.

"Hey," I said as she pulled the bowl across the table.

She pushed her bowl to my side, glanced into her new bowl, and grinned.

"You're a little shit," she said.

I shrugged my shoulders and grinned.

Having Sunday dinner at my mother's house was something I would have loved to adopt as tradition. I hoped Blake would agree, seeing some value in having a peaceful meal with a family of sorts. I realized nothing would be able to change his past, and no one could or would ever replace his parents, but my mother and I could sure provide him with as much love and good food as anyone would ever be able to accept.

"I want you to love Blake," I said.

207

She gazed beyond the shrimp filled fork she was lifting to her mouth. "I already do."

"Did you ever love Stephen?" I asked.

She poked the fork into her mouth, pulled the empty tines past her lips, and chewed the pasta. After a moment she took a drink of water, swallowed, and cleared her throat.

"Sorry, I didn't want to choke on my food. No, honey, I hated Stephen. That's why I never asked you to have him over. He disgusted me with the way he treated you. I'm so relieved you finally left him," she said.

I widened my eyes. "Hated him? Like hated him?"

"More than a spider," she said as she poked her fork into her bowl.

"I love you," I said with a laugh.

"And I love the two of you. Now make this thing happen," she said.

"I'll do my best," I said.

"That's all you can do," she said. "I sure hope he agrees."

I sat, staring at my mother, realizing just how much she truly loved me. Children deserved to get unconditional love from their parents, and to be treated with care and respect at all times.

And, as much as I took her love of me for granted when I was young, I now appreciated it with all of my being.

And I loved her back.

Equally.

BLAKE

"It isn't that I don't like it," I said. "It's just that I don't like it as much as this."

"Ohhh….kay," Riley grunted between thrusts.

We had been fucking for almost an hour, in every conceivable position imaginable. After trying almost everything once, we were back at what had become one of my favorites, doggy style.

I pulled her hair taught and pounded my cock in and out of her pussy, amazed that something didn't break. As the sound of my hips slapping against her ass filled the small bedroom, I began to wonder if her neighbors could hear us.

I didn't care. There was nothing or no one that would be able to stop me from fucking her. I was in love with her, and I was in love with fucking her. No differently than a kid who had received a new bicycle for Christmas, I was spending every spare moment I had riding it.

Or, riding her.

"You're….going….to…pull…my…hair out," she said in between breaths as I continued to pound away.

"Want me to let go?" I asked.

"No!" she bellowed.

I reached back with my left hand and slapped the side of her ass. As odd as it seemed at first, it was something I learned I enjoyed immensely, and as further proof Riley and I were meant to be together, it was something she enjoyed equally as well.

I reached around the left side of her waist, and with my finger still stinging from slapping her ass, began to rub her clit while I pushed myself as deep as I was able. As I held my hips tight to her ass and my swollen rod deep within her dripping wet pussy. I strummed a tune against her swollen love button.

"Blake!" she screamed. "Pah…Pah…Please staaahhhhp."

Her cries went unanswered and I continued as if they didn't pertain to me. Making her reach climax as many times as I could and as quickly as I was able had become my newfound pleasure. Pleasing her pleased me.

I rubbed the swollen nub, pulling her hair tight enough to cause her to arch her back in hope of a little relief. As I felt her begin to contract around my throbbing rod, I slid my finger inside of her and held it deeply, pressing my knuckle against the top of my cock. She wailed in pleasure as I began once again to pound myself in and out of her tight twat.

"I came," she wailed. "Please….stop."

"So you're going to let some novice out-fuck you?" I asked as I repeatedly thrust myself in and out of her.

Her arms folded up and she collapsed onto the bed.

"Fine. But I'm going to get one more out of you," I said flatly.

I slowly pulled myself from inside of her, gripped her waist in my hands, and raised her ass slightly. With her chest still pressed into the bed and her head buried in the comforter, I situated my face between her ass cheeks and buried my tongue inside of her dripping pussy.

"Blaaaaake!" she cried.

I worked my finger in and out of her wetness as I licked and slurped her juices. After what seemed like only a matter of minutes, she raised her head slightly and her breathing changed to short choppy breaths.

"I'm…"

I flicked the tip of my tongue across her clit and into her pussy. Over and over, I repeated to process of licking her clit and then forcing my tongue as deep as possible.

Her body began to shake in my hands. I buried my face deeper between her thighs.

As I felt her quivering in my hands I continued, until she cried out into the room expressing pleasure I was sure only I could provide.

After she collapsed onto the bed, she rolled to her side and stared.

"What?" I asked.

"I created a monster," she said.

I grinned.

"Life was so peaceful before you fucked me the first time," she said.

"You sad we started?" I asked.

"Don't be stupid," she said.

I gazed into her eyes and for a moment became lost, loving her looks, her beauty, her personality, and her wit. As my eyes came back into focus, I realized she was almost doing the same, staring at me blankly. In a short time she grinned.

She puckered her lips and raised her head slightly. "Kiss me.".

"You'll get pussy all over your face," I said.

"Good pussy," she said with a laugh.

'The best," I said as I pressed my lips to hers.

And, in my mind, not only was it the best, but it was the only pussy on this earth.

RILEY

Leaving home young and living a life under the watchful eye of someone more concerned with controlling me than loving me left me without any of the friends I had when I was in school. In the four years while I was separated from all of my former friends, they found lovers of their own, some had children, and others moved away.

Stevie was brash, crude, and annoying at times.

But she was very easy to like.

She moved her foot away from the switch, lifted the tattoo machine from his chest, and glared at him. "If you keep whining and squirming around like a little bitch, I'm going to have Riley paint your fingernails, put lipstick on you, and kick your ass out into the street. Fuck, can you just shut up?"

Lying flat on his back on the table, her client was very thin, pale, and appeared to be not much over the eighteen year old age requirement. He opened his eyes and gazed back at her.

"It fucking hurts," he whined.

"It's supposed to hurt, it's a fucking tattoo. Maybe you should have got a dove on your ass instead of an eagle on your chest," she said.

He nodded his head and blinked his eyes. "I think I'm okay. Go ahead."

She stepped on the pedal. The machine began to buzz, and she pressed the needle against his skin. After a few seconds, he wailed out into the room and waved his hands in the air.

"Stop, stop, stop…I'm done," he said.

She had started the tattoo merely minutes before, and had just begun the outline of the eagles head.

"You're fucking kidding, right?" she asked.

"No," he said as he sat up in the chair. "I'm done."

She stood from her stool, still gripping the tattoo machine in her hand. "Giving up, huh?"

"Yea, I can't take it. What do I owe you?" he asked.

"Hundred bucks," she said.

"A hundred for *this*?" he said as he pointed to his chest.

"You fucking pussy. Do you think that eagle drew itself? I drew that motherfucker by hand. It took me almost four fucking hours. You didn't leave a deposit, so yeah. A hundred bucks is cheap," she seethed.

He shook his head.

She pressed her foot against the pedal and leaned forward as if she was going to poke him with the buzzing needle.

"Fine," he said as he reached for his wallet.

After handing her a handful of money, he reached for his shirt. As he walked toward the door, he pulled the shirt over his head, mumbling to himself the entire time. I wondered as he pushed the door open, stepped out onto the side walk, and turned away just how many people were wandering the streets with half-finished tattoos on their skin.

"Wow, that was funny," I said.

"What a twat," she said as she pulled her gloves off and tossed them in the trash.

"I can't believe he didn't even make it fifteen minutes," I said.

"More like five," she said over her shoulder as she tossed the inkwell into the trash.

With her hair now colored grey from her roots to the tips, she seemed so much different than when we met. After commenting on her newest choice in color - which I actually liked a lot - she warned me not to become too attached to anything she did with her hair, as she changed the color no less than once a month.

"I know you said you're going to change it, but I really like your hair," I said.

She glanced in my direction and grinned. "Thanks. I like yours too. It always looks so healthy."

"It's almost brown," I said.

She shook her head and stared. "It's blonde as fuck."

"If I didn't color it, it'd be brown. Like almost black," I said.

"No shit? I like it blonde. It looks good," she said with a nod.

She glanced around the shop. Thursday mornings were normally busy, but with Stevie's cancelled appointment and Blake in Winfield with Jackson until noon, the shop was completely empty.

"Thanks," I said.

"Let me braid it for you," she said as she reached for my hair.

"Uhhm, okay," I said.

"We're going to be sitting here with our thumbs in our asses until somebody walks in," she said.

"Come over here and sit," she said as she sat down in her chair and patted the stool beside her.

I sat down in the stool, and almost immediately she began to run her fingers through my hair. It reminded me of when I was a little girl and my mother would braid my hair before school. On the occasions she chose to do so, I always felt special and spent the entire day believing I was much more beautiful than any of the other girls in my class.

As she separated each section of hair, I wondered what it might look like when she was done. My hair had grown quite long, and was at least a foot past my shoulders in length. I closed my eyes and smiled as the music played and she quietly continued to tug against my hair and fold it into place.

"So you and Blake are quite the couple," she said.

I opened my eyes. "Why do you say that?"

"You're like teenagers the way you look at each other," she said as she continued to work her fingers through my hair.

"We're in love," I said.

"Well, it shows. It's cute. Makes me want to have a guy who's normal," she said.

I turned my head slightly to the side and shifted my eyes until she came into view. "What happened to Vince?"

She slapped her hand against the side of my head. "Turn around."

I faced forward, laughing to myself at her harsh nature and wondering just how much of it was a simply a show and how much was genuine.

"What happened to Vince?" I asked again.

"I heard you, hold on a minute," she said as she worked her way around the back of my head.

"He came in, got three knuckle tats, and we talked. That was it. Didn't even offer to take me for a ride," she said.

"That sucks," I said.

Stevie was beautiful. If she didn't say anything, most men would be intimidated by her beauty, and probably wouldn't even think they had a chance of ever being with her. When she opened her mouth, a long string of expletives soon followed, and eventually the conversations always went to the subject of sex, regardless of whether she was in the presence of a man, a woman, or both. I suspected her outgoing personality and her sailor mouth prevented her from finding the man she wanted, but I feared telling her so.

"Yeah, sucks balls. Oh well, there'll always be another," she said as her hands moved along the right side of my head.

"So, what exactly are you doing?" I asked.

"About what?" she responded.

I chuckled lightly. "With my hair?"

"You'll see," she said. "Almost done. You're a pretty bitch, just so you know."

"You're a pretty bitch," I said over my shoulder.

She slapped the left side of my head sharply. "Turn the fuck around."

I reached up and scratched my head where she had slapped me. A few minutes and a few tugs later, she tapped me on the shoulder.

"All done," she said.

I stood from my seat, pressed my hands against my hair, and felt the braids. As I stepped in front of the mirror I inhaled a sharp breath.

"Oh my God, it's beautiful. What…" I stared at myself in the mirror as I raised my hands to my head. "What's it called?"

"Waterfall braid. It's easy," she said as she walked up behind me.

"I love it," I said.

"Can you teach me?" I asked.

She shook her head. "Sorry. You're too much of a ding dong to understand."

"I'm serious," I said.

"So am I," she said with a laugh as she turned away.

"I can't wait till Blake sees it," I said.

"Neither can I," she responded.

I turned to face her. "Why's that?"

She shrugged her shoulders. "I don't know. It's just, you know, seeing you two makes me kind of happy or whatever. I almost trick myself into thinking one day I might have something similar. Not with some pinch-faced rat like Blake, but some guy that at least acts like him."

I scrunched my nose and narrowed my eyes. "Pinch-faced?"

She shrugged her shoulders again and grabbed her pink mannequin head, the one labeled "Bad as Fuck." As she placed it at the front of her drawing table, she glanced over her shoulder.

"Grab your stool and come here. I'll show you how to do it," she said.

I grinned and turned toward the front of the shop. As I walked back with the stool I realized Stevie wasn't much different than me, or anyone else for that matter. She was what my mother had always called an M&M.

Hard on the outside, and sweet once you cracked the outer shell.

As we wove the pink hair together into a beautiful waterfall braid, I couldn't help but smile.

Having Stevie as a friend was best described by the writing on the face of her expressionless mannequin head.

Bad as Fuck.

BLAKE

There were five men standing in a group in front of me, all of which looked like they were ready to go to war. One, a former Marine, one no less than six foot six - and muscle from head to toe, one with his face covered in a long beard - and rocking an awesome southern drawl, Axton, and Jackson.

"So here's the deal. There isn't one of the fellas that wouldn't go take care of this fucker, but not if you went along. There's one hell of a brotherhood amongst us, but it is amongst *us*," Axton explained.

I nodded my head.

"So here's what we've got. Toad, Biscuit, Otis, Big Jack, and me. Well, and you. We're it. You're good with Jack, so you're good with me. These other fellas volunteered because, well, because they're who they are. This is a damned strange series of circumstances, and normally there wouldn't be any of us that'd be doing a fucking thing in your presence, but here we are. And Jack may or may not have some things he wants to tell you, I'm not sure, but I need to make good and god damned sure you're not going to get soft on us, or I'll leave your happy little tattooing ass here," Axton growled.

"I won't go soft," I said.

Axton shook his head and crossed his arms in front of his massive chest. I'd never been in the presence of anyone quite as intimidating as he was. His glare alone was enough to cause almost any man to understand turning away and running was his only viable option.

"You say that," he said. "But until the shit gets real, you never know."

"I know," I said.

"Time will tell," he said.

I nodded my head and glanced around the garage.

"Pay fucking attention," he grunted.

I shifted my eyes toward him and nodded my head again.

He sighed and shook his head as if frustrated with me. "So, the clock's been moved up, and after our own little investigation, we're going tomorrow mid-day. He's got a church service in the evening, and we're going to get him right after that."

"I'm good with that," I said.

"One of the fellas is renting a Ryder van under his name and staying home with his wife so he's got a solid alibi, and we're taking it down there. It'll be a shitty little ride, but…"

"We're not riding?" I asked.

He sighed, glanced around the group of men, and flexed his massive biceps. "You interrupt me again, and I'll toss your little ass out in the street."

"Sorry."

"No," he said. We're not riding. Too much risk. And we need somewhere to toss his ass. We'll go over details tomorrow. Meeting here at two o'clock tomorrow. You good with that?"

I nodded my head. "Yep."

"And what's said here, stays here. Not even your pretty Ol' Lady," he said.

"Understood," I said.

"Big Jack?" Axton said.

Jackson glanced at me, inhaled a deep breath, and sighed. As he gazed down at his boots, the men all did the same. I felt he'd shared something with them he had yet to share with me, and wondered what it may be.

"I uhhm…I talked to my sis the other day after we met. You remember Syd?" he asked, still staring down at his boots.

"Yeah, I remember her," I said.

"Well, let's just say you weren't the only one. This isn't just about you anymore, I want to make sure that's understood," he said as he glanced up from his boots.

I swallowed heavily and stared. As his gaze met mine I noticed his eyes looked distant, tired, and every bit of angry.

I wet my lips and nodded once. "Understood."

"This deal will make you or break you," he said. "I owe you for making me aware of what happened to Syd, I damned sure do. But if you go soft on me, I'll leave you there right beside that cock sucker. And that, little man, is a promise."

"It's not going to happen, Jackson," I said in an assuring tone.

I shifted my eyes to each of the men, making a point to maintain eye contact with each of them.

"It's not going to happen," I repeated.

And I meant every word I said.

RILEY

I dug in my closet, finding every card, note, piece of jewelry, and trinket Stephen had ever given me. Some dated back to the summer of my junior year in high school, and although at the time I received them they meant the world to me, now they meant less than nothing.

I glanced behind me. A twelve inch high mound of treasures in a pile roughly three feet across. I stood, stared down at the mess, and shook my head. After walking into the kitchen and getting two trash bags, I separated the paper from the jewelry and few articles of clothing.

I walked back into the kitchen and got the lighter fluid for the grill and the matches. Proudly, I walked into the driveway and poured the bag of clothes and letters into a pile. After dousing it in fluid, I set it afire and walked back into the house.

A small pile of rings, bracelets, necklaces, earrings, and perfume lay on the floor. I scooped the items into my hands and transferred them to the bag. I glanced around the room and grinned at the thought of nothing in my home being a result of meeting him.

I walked to the garage, got in my car, and backed out over the still smoldering pile of debris.

Within fifteen minutes, I had driven to a depressed area of town. A Woman waiting at the crosswalk for the light to turn studied my car. A BMW M6 probably wasn't something she saw every day. I rolled down my passenger window and smiled.

"Hi, I'm Riley. Want some jewelry?" I asked.

She walked up to the window and stared.

"Would you like some jewelry? It's real. Gold, diamonds, all kinds of stuff," I said cheerily.

She furrowed her weathered brow. "Steal it?"

"Seriously? No, my ex-boyfriend gave it to me. You can go pawn it and get some money. Maybe buy something nice," I said as I tossed my head toward the bag.

She shrugged her shoulders, appearing to still be uncertain if it was a trick. I reached in the rear seat and produced the bag. As I hoisted it into the air, it was apparent the bag was filled with twenty ponds of treasure.

Her eyes widened and she reached for the bag. "Give it here."

I handed her the bag and grinned.

As I rolled up the window and drove away, I laughed at the thought of Stephen actually doing something nice for someone for once in his life.

And he didn't even know it.

BLAKE

I had never known love. Although I was quite certain both of my parents loved me, I had very little recollection of them being in my life. Most of what I believed I remembered was more than likely false memories manufactured by my mind in an effort to prove to me they existed at some point and time in my life.

The remaining portion of my childhood was filled with children, adults, and confusion, but not love. As I reached adolescence, I was curious about women, relationships, and sex; but for many reasons I never acted on any of the ideas my curiosity presented.

When I finally reached a point I felt I was able to be in a relationship and possibly provide a woman with the care, affection, and love a relationship required, the fear of failure far outweighed what I believed the possible gains might be. Time seemed to pass all too quickly once I reached adulthood. The constant searching for whatever it is that we as adults seek, the striving to succeed, and the filling our days with events to reassure us we're accomplishing exactly what it is we're supposed to seemed to consume me. And, one day I looked in the mirror, and the failure I feared I may become looked back at me.

I then chose to tattoo myself heavily, making me seem repulsive to others on the surface, hoping all along that the tattoos would cause rejection by all who exposed only to what their eyes were able to see. It seemed to work, and my life of solitude which followed was confirmation of me being distasteful to those who exposed themselves to me.

Loneliness followed hand in hand with my life of isolation, so my mind developed a world of fantasy in which I was able to live without repercussion.

Without rejection.

Without heartache.

And without pain.

If I was forced to look at myself with a critical eye, my alcoholism would be the only true fault I felt I possessed, and it was not as much of a fault as it was a disease. I began drinking when I was thirteen, much earlier than most, but I had always felt it wasn't quite early enough. I found an odd comfort in knowing once I decided to change my life and stop drinking, I met Riley.

At almost the exact time I stopped drinking, she packed her bags and left an abusive relationship. Six months later, we met. Be it by happenstance or by some strange twist of fate I didn't know, but it really didn't matter in the least. What did matter was that she was able to easily fit into my life where so many others weren't.

She stood in the kitchen carving the ends from the strawberries and watching them fall into the sink. Each time she grabbed a strawberry from the container she lifted the knife with the opposite hand, cut off the end, and tossed each respective piece in different directions. The fluid movements of her arms appeared to be mechanized and almost perfect. As her arms moved back and forth with a certain grace, I studied her tattoos. The bold colors seemed to be more prominent in the natural light of the kitchen. I stood at the edge of the doorway leading to the kitchen, behind her and out of her view, and admired the work I had done on her arm.

For the rest of her life she would be marked by my mind's creations, a piece of artwork unlike anything else, and something unique to her. I never tattooed the same design on two people for many reasons, and I prided myself in the fact I had not. After a few minutes of admiring her grace, beauty, I cleared my throat.

She glanced over her shoulder.

"Come here," I said.

She glanced over her shoulder and grinned. "Just a minute."

There was so much I wanted to say, but didn't dare. I knew the next day I was going to be headed out of town into a situation that could easily go in an unfavorable direction. Nonetheless, I knew it was something I needed to do, and in the end, Riley and I would both be better as a result after it was all behind me.

I wasn't only doing it for me; I was doing it for us.

For our growth as a couple.

I anxiously took the few steps that separated us and wrapped my arms around her, resting my hands at her waist. With my chin resting on her shoulder, I watched as she finished cleaning the strawberries. As she held the strainer under the faucet and ran cold water over the fruit, I reached into the basket and pinched one of the berries between my thumb and forefinger.

Silently, I lifted it to her mouth. She opened her mouth, accepted the fruit, and wrapped her lips around the tips of my fingers. As she sucked the sticky juice from the tips of my fingers, I leaned forward and tilted my head to the side.

She shifted her eyes to meet mine and grinned. I held her gaze and smiled in return.

I blindly reached for the strainer. After fumbling for another piece of fruit, I eventually found one and lifted it to her mouth. Again, her lips parted, wrapped around my fingers, and sucked the juices from my fingertips.

I pressed my hands to her sides, pushed them along the length of her body, and past her hips. As my hands reached the bottom of her shirt, I grasped it in my fingers and slowly pulled it upward. As the shirt slowly revealed the bare skin of her back, she lifted her arms over her head, allowing me to remove it completely.

I pressed my chin against the side of her neck and kissed her under the chin. As my mouth moved along her jaw line, she tilted her head rearward and closed her eyes. Gently kissing the soft skin underneath her ear, I reached for her bra and unclasped it. As I continued to kiss along her neck and eventually her shoulder, I slid my hands beneath her dangling bra and cupped her breasts in my palms.

With her head still tilted back and her eyes closed, she moaned as I massaged her flesh in my fingers. I dragged my teeth along the base of her neck and across her shoulder, my tongue darting across every inch of her skin as I did so.

I released her breasts, pushed my hands against her skin, and slowly slid my fingers into the waist of her shorts. Her moaning increased as my fingers followed the crease from her hips to her wet mound.

I curled my middle finger upward and into her wetness. Slowly and gently I worked in and out of her tight wet slit, pressing slightly further each time. Within a few seconds it was buried deep inside of her and the palm of my hands was covered in her satisfaction.

She reached for the waist of her shorts, unfastened them, and pushed them along her thighs. As she continued to fight against the unwilling garment, I turned her to face me and kissed along her neck, past each of her breasts, and onto her stomach. As she playfully kicked her shorts to the side, I knelt in front of her and gripped her bare ass in my hands.

I opened my mouth, extended my tongue, and gazed upward. As our eyes met, I grinned. She spread her stance slightly, stepped forward, and pressed her sweet wet flesh against my mouth. Eagerly, I licked her. With each stroke of my tongue, she pulled away slightly, only to return for taste of what I had to offer her.

After a few minutes of my tongue carefully exploring her every crevice and fold, she reached down and gripped my head in her hands. In perfect rhythm we continued; her pulling my head into her slightly, and me licking with precision. Her moaning acted as the only warning of her body's intended release.

As she bellowed into the room, I flicked my tongue against the swollen nub at the top of her wetness, forcing her even further into the heavenly cloud her mind had certainly taken her. The few spasmodic thrusts of her hips that followed provided a sense of satisfaction that I had satisfied her as much as I had hoped.

I released her from my grasp and slowly stood. She gazed down and followed my hands as I unbuckled my belt, lowered my jeans, and removed my shorts. As I removed my shirt, she grinned, but did not speak. I placed a hand against her shoulder, turned her around, and directed her to the sink. As I gazed over her shoulder and into the basket of strawberries, I pressed my hand against her back. Without hesitation, she bent at the waist, resting her stomach against the edge of the counter.

I gathered her hair in my hand, held it firmly, and guided myself between her legs. As I felt her warmth encompass my swollen shaft, I pressed my chest against her back and pulled her hair tight with my hand.

As I slowly and predictably worked myself in and out, she grunted softly with each stroke. I sank my teeth into the side of her neck, pulled her hair rearward further, and pushed myself even deeper.

Her back arched slightly, and her mouth opened. Slowly, as I held myself in place deep within her, her eyes fell closed and she tightened around me. As I felt my love for her release in short bursts of pleasure, I released her hair.

She moaned out into the room.

With our bodies pressed against each other and our skin affixed slightly from the sweat we had created, I held her in my arms. As I kissed along her shoulder and onto her neck, she turned to the side and parted her lips slightly.

I closed my eyes and leaned into her, pressing my lips against hers. A long, slow, sensual kiss followed.

I rested my chin against her shoulder, realizing it was where we had started only a short time before. As I closed my eyes and gave thanks for Riley's existence, I felt her finger tap lightly against my lips.

With my eyes still closed, I opened my mouth.

A piece of the roughly textured fruit was pushed past my lips and into my mouth. As I bit into the sweet fruit, it acted as a reminder that not all things are as they appear.

Sometimes the repulsive surface acts as a disguise of what may be the sweetest of life's offerings.

RILEY

After logging the appointment into the computer, I turned toward the back of the shop. Stevie sat on the edge of her stool finishing a tattoo she had been working on for a few hours. The woman getting tattooed had a very interesting story, and after hearing it, I loved the concept of her tattoo, feeling it would depict something that was extremely important in her life, and how everything came to work out. I had seen the outline of the tattoo, and walked back a few times during the shading, but was eager to see it once it was finished.

"How's it coming along?" I asked as I walked to Stevie's side.

"Have a look," she said as she nodded her head toward the piece.

The scantily dressed woman holding a set of scales in one hand and a sword with the other all done in black and grey appeared to be finished. It looked like a photograph. The quality of the realism in Stevie's work amazed me, and this particular piece was a nothing short of a masterpiece.

"Justice," the woman said as she glanced up.

Dressed in jean shorts, Chuck's, and a tee shirt, she looked like she could have been my sister, only a few years older, but not much.

"It's…" I stared down at the tattoo. "It's uhhm. It's amazing."

"I love it," she said as she shifted her eyes toward Stevie and grinned.

"Let me get it wiped down and have one last look," Stevie said.

After wiping the tattoo clean, Stevie inspected it thoroughly. Satisfied the piece needed no touch-up work, she stood from her stool and smiled.

"Looks awesome," Stevie said as she pulled off her gloves.

"So, you said after almost ten years, he finally got out of prison, and you waited all that time?" I asked.

She nodded her head and smiled. "Love is a powerful thing."

"It sure is," I said.

"Were you here when she said her Ol' Man's Jackson?" Stevie asked.

"Oh, wow. I guess not," I said.

Stevie nodded her head. "Yep. He did ten fucking years on a bullshit conspiracy charge. ATF set his ass up. So ten years later, the Ol' Lady of the president of the club he rides with now hears about his case, files an appeal, and gets him out of prison. He gets out of the joint and rides with the club. Story gets a lot better, but I'll let her tell ya."

"So, Jackson? The big guy with the big arms?" I asked.

"Sounds like him," she said.

"He and Blake grew up together," I said.

"That's what he said. Sad how they met, but I'm glad they found each other," she said.

"Me too. Blake doesn't really have any friends. He doesn't trust people," I said.

"Where is he now?" she asked.

"Kansas City, at some tattooing convention that came up," I responded. "And Jackson?"

"Out riding with the fellas. It's like a disease," she said with a laugh.

"You ride?" I asked.

She stood from the chair and smiled. "As much as I can. Love it, personally."

"Me too," I said.

"So, you going to tell me the story?" I asked.

"Sure," she said as she sat down in her seat. "I never get tired of telling it."

"Jackson Shephard never breaks a promise. We met ten years ago when he walked into a bar when a guy was groping me. He never knew me, had ever seen me, or anything. So, I'm telling this guy to leave me alone, and he steps in. He beat the shit out of the guy and gave him a lecture on respecting women. I walked out of the bar with my panties in a puddle behind me," she said.

I laughed and nodded my head, eager to hear more.

"So, he goes on to tell me he doesn't fuck around, and he didn't want sex. He was single, but convincing him to give me a chance was impossible. After a long - and I do mean long - courtship, we ended up together," she paused, sighed, and smiled.

"He had an ATF agent working undercover in his club, and the man convinced him one night in a club when he was drunk to admit he'd kill a rival member if they threatened the club. It was male bravado bullshit, but the court saw it differently. They gave him life in prison. When he left the courtroom, I asked him to promise me he'd never see me again. He wouldn't do it. They drug him out of there, and I cried for six months," she paused, wiped her eyes, and gazed down at the floor.

She shifted her eyes upward and focused on the doorway. "Sorry, it still makes me teary-eyed thinking about it. Anyway, he spent almost ten years in prison. He was convinced his life was over, and he was convinced having so much as a visitor would drag them down into the hell he was living in, so he removed everyone from his visiting list and began his life of living alone."

"I moved around the country, madly in love with him just as much as the day he left, knowing one day everything would be alright. Don't ask me how, but I knew. I knew one day," she paused and wiped the tears from her cheeks with the tip of her finger.

"I knew one day my Jackson…I knew he'd come back to me." She nodded her head and wiped her finger on her thigh.

"So. I was in Las Vegas. I'd just opened a restaurant there. It was my third in the ten years he was away. I was talking to a food critic, and I saw this man standing in the distance crying. It was sunny, and the sun was in my eyes, but I thought for a second I was going crazy. So I sat there talking to her and staring at him. And he slowly walked my direction…"

She paused and sighed heavily.

"Ten years. And it all came rushing back. He'd been brought back on an appeal, won, and was released free and clear. He rode his bike around the country trying to find me, and finally he did. He gave me a kiss, and here we are," she said as she spread her arms wide.

"Oh wow. That's awesome," I said.

"Gives me goosebumps," Stevie said.

"What was your name again?" I asked.

She stood from her chair. "Em. Call me Em."

"Riley, it's nice to meet you. I like that story," I said.

"I like telling it," she said. She turned toward Stevie. "What do I owe you?"

"Tell you what. What do you say, Riley? Can we lock this bitch up a little early?" Stevie asked.

I shrugged my shoulders. "Uhhhm…"

"Girl's night out," Stevie said.

"Oh wow. Uhhm," I paused and looked at the clock.

The thought of a girl's night out was exciting. I hadn't done anything with girlfriends since my senior year in high school. I tried unsuccessfully to hide my excitement as I turned toward Stevie.

"Don't tell Blake what time we locked it up," I said as I shifted my eyes back and forth between them.

Stevie shrugged.

Em shrugged.

And I locked the door behind me.

BLAKE

God is not evil. Men who hide behind the word of God, using it as a shield to protect them from the questions which would normally arise in the absence of God's word they so righteously spit at each person in their path, however, define evil.

"If God didn't want you to, He wouldn't have sent me to save you. The children of this earth are treasures, and each and every one is formed by God's hands with a gift. The gift each child possesses should be shared, and shared so that it may be seen in the eyes of God. Your gift to Him in appreciation of the gift He graced you with. This, Blake, is your gift. And through me, the hand of God, it should be shared," he said.

I was eight at the time, and wanted nothing more than to please him.

"My gift?" I asked.

He squeezed my shoulder lightly and nodded his head. "Yes, this is your gift. The pain you will feel is a reminder of the sacrifice Jesus made on the cross for you. You're strong Blake, so, so much stronger than the rest. God's gift to you was strength. Tremendous strength. Do you know what tremendous means?"

I nodded my head. "Like Superman?"

"Yes, like Superman. Blake, God made you this way for a reason. He formed you with his hands, providing you with something special. And God has sent me here to test your strength and send a message

237

back to Him, and it will be sent through my test of you and a test of your exhibition of the strength God has graced you with. Can you please God?" he asked.

I nodded my head again. "I think so."

He squeezed my shoulder and crouched down almost even with me. "What happens if you disappoint God?"

I lowered my head and pointed at my feet. He had taught me the earth beneath me was a fiery pit of hell reserved for those who disappointed God by rejecting his word and his wishes.

"You are so right. In hell you'd burn. You make me proud, Blake. You make me proud. Are you ready to please God?" he asked as he stood.

I nodded my head.

His son walked between us, lifted my hands, and guided me to the edge of the stairs. I remember feeling an odd sense of guilt, at least initially, that the rest of the family wasn't present for my portrayal of strength, especially if it was a message directly to God. For me to prove myself, and not share the blessed news with the family made me feel slightly cheated.

He handed me a bible. As I accepted it in my hands, I grinned. I didn't have a bible of my own, and holding one made me feel important and powerful.

"If the pain becomes more than you are able to withstand, bite into the Bible, it will provide strength," he said.

As I clutched the Bible and nodded my head, his son removed my clothes. I remember feeling dirty, silly, and embarrassed all at the same time.

But.

If it was God's will, I knew I needed to make it mine.

As the pain shot through me like a bolt of lightning, I glanced up at his son. With my face filled with wonder, fear, and surprise, I wanted an answer.

Something.

He released one of my wrists and reached for the Bible I held in my shaking hand. As he helped me lift it to my mouth he nodded his head once, reassuring me it was okay.

And into the sacred book I sank my teeth.

RILEY

We sat on the same bench beside the lake where we first shared our secrets. The sun began to set in the distance, and the late evening clouds blocked the few remaining minutes of sunshine, but provided an extremely colorful sunset. Blake's tattoo convention must have been very relaxing for him, because he seemed satisfied with everything since he returned.

"I talked to Doc Racine on the phone this morning," he said as he gazed toward the western sky.

"About…"

"Well, I don't think I need to go back. It all started because of my past, and now that we've written that letter, and worked out the entire sex thing, there's really nothing left," he said.

"You think? Really? Like never go back?" I asked, excited about his progress with everything in life.

"Maybe not. We'll see, I suppose, but I'm feeling pretty good about everything," he said.

His face looked healthy. I knew he rarely slept an entire night, and often stayed up drawing until very late, but to Blake, it was his therapy. Tonight, however, he looked like he had received full night's sleep, and he seemed to be at peace staring out at the sunset.

"Are you okay?" I asked.

"You know," he said as continued to gaze blankly at the horizon.

He turned toward me and smiled. "I'm really good, Riley. Really good. I uhhm. That's why I wanted to come here. Just to talk and relax. It's peaceful here. It just seems like this is where everything started to be, I don't know, fixed."

"I like it here, too."

"So, I talked to Jackson this morning," he said.

"Oh, yeah, and?" I asked.

"Well, you know. Clubs never ask a person to be a member or prospect. Never happens. But uhhm. If a guy asks them about being a member, then they offer everything up. You know, the process and all. But it always starts from an outsider asking," he said.

I nodded my head. "Okay."

"Well, I made the mistake of asking how a guy becomes a member," he said.

"Oh. Wow. Uhhm, what happened?" I asked.

"He turned sideways on the bench and placed his hand on my thigh. "They asked me to become a prospect."

I swallowed heavily. From my talk with Em in the bar, she shared with me how the club had become a family for Jackson, and that it was the best thing that ever happened to him. She also explained the level of secrecy the men have regarding the club and club business. As much as I hated to admit it, I was excited for Blake to possibly become a member of something like a motorcycle club, and I felt it would provide me with several new girlfriends.

"What did you say?" I asked.

"Told him I'd think about it," he said.

"Well, you ride, you love to ride, and you're covered in tattoos. Hell, you don't even own a car. And you don't have a family. I think you're perfect for it," I said as I reached for his hand.

"Do you?" he asked.

I nodded my head. "I do. And I'd be proud of you if you did. And you know how my mom feels about those guys. In her eyes, they can't do any wrong. She just loves Axton."

"You be proud?" he asked.

"Who wouldn't? Yes, I really would," I said.

"Well, I'll sleep on it," he said. "And we'll talk again, okay?"

"Okay," I said with a smile.

"And I've got something," I said.

"Let's hear it. What, you catch the shop on fire?" he asked.

I laughed. "No. My uhhm. My mom, she wants to start a tradition, and she wants to know if you're interested."

"Depends on what it is," he said.

"She wants to have Sunday dinner at her house every Sunday. You know, like a family." I said.

Slowly, he twisted his forearm half around, gazed at the line tattooed across his wrist, and stared. "That'd be really nice," he said as he glanced up.

I jumped up from the bench. "You mean you'll do it?"

"Yeah. It'd be nice," he said.

"Oh wow. Mom's just gonna die. She's going to be so happy. You realize this is like every Sunday, right?" I asked.

He stood from the bench and wrapped his arms around me. "Yes, I understand. And it sounds perfect. Like a family."

"Yes," I said.

A tear welled in my eye and slowly crept down my cheek at the thought of Blake having something he could call a family.

"A family," I said as I wiped my finger across my cheek.

"Let's go see her," he said.

"My mom?" I asked excitedly.

He nodded his head.

"Okay," I said as I reached down and grabbed my helmet.

"Meet me at the bike," he said. "I've got to do something really quick."

"Okay," I said.

It seemed strange for him to ask me to walk away, but if it was what he needed, I wanted to provide it. As I sat on the curb beside the bike and gazed down the hill at the lake, I watched as Blake reached into his pocket, pulled something out, and tossed it into the middle of the lake.

I couldn't tell for sure against the setting sun, but it looked like his cross.

After a moment, he walked up to the bike and smiled a huge smile. "Ready?"

I nodded my head and stood. "What did you throw away?"

He gazed down at his boots for a moment. As he shifted his eyes upward, he responded.

"My past," he said.

And I fully believed him.

EPILOGUE

The young blonde walked in to the dining room with the platters of food and placed them on the table. The elder woman stared down at the food and shook her head. After a moment, she glanced upward and grinned.

"I have no idea on why you insisted cooking so much food, Riley. This is ridiculous," she said.

"Not ridiculous," the younger woman responded.

"It certainly is. This is a waste," she said as she tilted her head toward the table filled with food.

"Believe me, it's not a waste," she assured her as she turned toward the kitchen.

"Are you expecting more?" the woman asked.

Inside the kitchen and out of sight, the girl grinned and shrugged her shoulders. "Guess we'll have to see."

"And why didn't you two come together? You have ridden here together every Sunday for months," the woman said.

"I don't know, mom," the young woman responded.

She carried two more platters of food to the dining room, grinning the entire way into the dining room. She knew there would be more guests coming to dinner, but she hoped to keep the surprise as long as she was able. She glanced at her watch.

By her estimate, they were fifteen minutes late as it was. As the elder woman stared down at the food and shook her head once more, a thunderous roar from out in the street began to shake the windows.

"What…" the elder woman said as she stood from her seat.

She walked to the window, pulled the curtains to the side and stared out into the street. She grinned at what she saw, glanced over her shoulder, and glared at the younger woman.

"You should have told me they were coming," she said.

The younger woman shrugged her shoulders and smiled. As far as she knew, the arrival of the six men and five women were the extent of the surprise.

As the motorcycles parked along the street in a row along the curb in front of the house, a petite woman with heavily tattooed arms and pink hair walked in through the back door. Her hands filled with two platters of grilled chicken, she carefully walked across the beige carpeting and toward the kitchen.

"This is the last of it," she shouted.

"Just give it here, Stevie. The cat's out of the bag, they're here," the elder woman said.

"Oh, okay," the petite woman responded as she held the platters at arm's length.

The front door opened and the men and women came into the home in couples, with the exception of one man who walked in alone.

The last man in the house differed slightly. On his leather vest the word "Prospect" was sewn into the patch on the back. As he entered the house he glanced at the elder woman, walked her direction, and hugged her in his arms.

"Sorry we're late, mom," he said.

"It's quite alright, Blake," she responded with a smile. "You brought my favorite crew. I'll forgive you."

Nervously, the young man glanced around the room. "Where's Riley?"

"Right here," the young woman responded from the kitchen.

After walking into the kitchen, the young man wrapped his arms around the blonde woman and kissed her on the lips. A short verbal exchange later they walked hand-in-hand into the dining area.

"Are we ready?" The elder woman asked. "Is everyone here?"

The blonde woman with the tattooed arm glanced around the room and counted silently. "Yes," she said. "They're all here."

"Who's saying grace?" the mother asked.

"I'll say it," the man with the patch identifying him as president said as he raised his hand.

The young man cleared his throat. "Wait," he said as he held his index finger in the air.

He turned to face the younger blonde woman. As she gazed into his eyes and smiled, wondering why he had stopped the blessing of the meal, he knelt down before her.

"Riley," he said. "I love you."

The young woman began to softly cry. Her mother joined in shedding a tear. As the younger of the two women wiped the tears from rolling down her cheek, the young man reached into his vest and removed a solitaire diamond ring.

"As God, mom, and my brothers and sisters are my witness, Riley Jaye Campbell, will you marry me?" he asked.

She nodded her head, cleared her throat, and spoke the two words she'd yearned to say for a lifetime.

"I will."

OTHER BOOKS BY SCOTT HILDRETH

Broken People (NA Fiction/Genre Fiction)
ERIC EAD TRILOGY: Baby Girl – Ruined, Baby Girl – Owned,
Baby Girl – Loved (D/s Romance)
Boxer Erotic Romance: Undefeated, Unstoppable, Unleashed,
Unbroken (Romantic Erotica)
The Alpha-Bet (Humorous Erotica)
Threefold (Romantic Erotica)
Karter (Military Romance)
Finding Parker (NA Fiction/Contemporary Romance)
Selected Sinners Series: Making the Cut, Taking the Heat, Otis,
HUNG, EX-CON (MC Romance)
Bodies Ink and Steel Series: Blurred Lines (Romantic Erotica)

UNDER PEN NAMES
The Tortured, by RU Dumm (Erotic Thriller/Dark Erotica)

www.ingramcontent.com/pod-product-compliance
Lightning Source LLC
Chambersburg PA
CBHW031426200626
46814CB00016B/2333